Percy Hetherington Fitzgerald

The Savoy Opera

and the Savoyards

Percy Hetherington Fitzgerald

The Savoy Opera
and the Savoyards

ISBN/EAN: 9783337311490

Printed in Europe, USA, Canada, Australia, Japan

Cover: Foto ©Andreas Hilbeck / pixelio.de

More available books at **www.hansebooks.com**

THE SAVOY OPERA

AND THE SAVOYARDS

BY

ERCY FITZGERALD, M.A., F.S.A.

'His eye begets occasion for his wit,
And every object that the one doth catch
The other turns to a mirth-moving jest'

WITH SIXTY ILLUSTRATIONS

London
CHATTO & WINDUS, PICCADILLY
1894

INSCRIBED

TO

GEORGE GROSSMITH

PREFACE

To the Savoy opera and its merry men playgoers are indebted for many an agreeable hour and innumerable laughter-moving quips. I have thought, therefore, that some record of this pleasant home of song and humour would be welcome, and have gathered together everything about the plays, authors, and performers that is likely to be interesting. This will be found à *propos*, as the Savoy opera might be considered almost a new form of entertainment, which the public has accepted cordially. The present moment is suitable for such a review, on account of the late *amoris redintegratio*, when the old merry combination has been started afresh.

I fancy the extracts given from the various operas will be found acceptable as agreeable *souvenirs* of the more entertaining episodes. The traffic of the stage is now so busy and so hurried that these lively passages are likely enough to have been forgotten.

I may add that I have received abundant assistance and, indeed, every information I desired, from the best sources—Mr. W. S. GILBERT and Mr. and Mrs. D'OYLY CARTE.

ATHENÆUM CLUB:
May 1894.

CONTENTS

LIST OF ILLUSTRATIONS

THE SAVOY OPERA

WHAT a fund of enjoyment the community owes to the brilliant pair who for nearly twenty years have regularly increased for all 'the public stock of harmless pleasure'! The pleasant humours of the Savoy have served to recreate us not only during the performance, but have even spread in mirthful ripples over the mosaic surface of social life. The pair have diffused a genuine hilarity and cheerfulness, and their conceits are so piquant and original that even as we recall them now we find the muscles relaxing. There are no obstreperous bursts of laughter such as are provoked by the buffoonery of the burlesque, but a vein of quiet, placid enjoyment akin to that of comedy.

Gilbert has had more influence on the theatre and on public taste than any writer of the time. No one has enjoyed such complete and overpowering success. No one has been the cause of such general mirth. He

B

has succeeded not in one department, but in many.   He
was asked to furnish Mrs. Bancroft with a short piece of
domestic but strong interest, and ' Sweethearts ' at once
secured a position in the *répertoire* which it has never
lost ; it even inspired the beautiful waltz air which is
associated with it.   This success in a trifle is evidence
of purpose and ability ; only a skilled hand knows
how to suit his means to an end.   It was the same
with 'Clarice,' written for Miss Anderson, and later
transferred to Miss Neilson.   Could there be a more
mirthful and satirical production than the ' Happy
Land,' written under the name of Tomline ?   He has
written comedies, popularised what he called the ' Fairy
Comedy,' or fairy tale, supplied farces, burlesques,
operas, tragedies, and melodramas.   He has written
stories of the kind that the ' literary man ' furnishes to
newspapers and magazines, with poems and humorous
ballads, and has passed judgment on the works of his
brethren as a dramatic critic.   He is, moreover, a clever
and spirited artist—witness his grotesque sketches in the
style of Thackeray.   This is a wonderful record of talent
and versatility.[1]

---

[1] The following is a fairly complete list of Gilbert's productions in
all dramatic departments : The *Bab Ballads*, begun (in *Fun*) 1861 ;
Dulcamara, burlesque, St. James's Theatre, 1866 ; *Robert the Devil*,
1868 ; *La Vivandière*, 1868 ; the *Princess* ; the *Palace of Truth*, Haymarket, November 1870 ; *Pygmalion and Galatea*, 1871 ; *Thespis,
or the Gods Grown Old*, 1871 ; the *Wicked World*, January 1873 ; the

Many of his works have become what are called 'stock pieces,' and are acted again and again all over the kingdom, the colonies, and America. 'Sweethearts,' 'Pygmalion and Galatea,' 'Creatures of Impulse,' 'Dan'l Druce,' 'Trial by Jury,' 'Comedy and Tragedy,' are in constant requisition. This is substantial praise, for there are not a dozen 'stock pieces' in the *répertoire*. Further, he has extraordinary business instincts. No literary man—or, at least, dramatist—since Dickens has made such a fortune or has turned it to such profit. He has built the Garrick Theatre, now leased to Mr. Hare, and which from its admirable situation is certain to prove a most valuable property. He is, moreover, a man of ready wit and furnishes cheerful company. He is, in short, one of the best specimens of a generally successful man, and I have dwelt to this extent upon his merits for the reason that we are often apt from familiarity to overlook such claims to our respect and emulation.

Gilbert has always been eager to shine in comedy,

Happy Land, 1873; *Sweethearts*, 1874; *Broken Hearts*, 1875; *Randall's Thumb*; *Tom Cobb*, 1875; *Thespis*, 1875; *Creatures of Impulse*; *Dan'l Druce*, 1876; *Trial by Jury*, 1876; the *Sorcerer*, 1877; *H.M.S. Pinafore*, 1878; the *Ne'er-do-weel*, 1878; *Gretchen*, 1879; the *Pirates of Penzance*, 1880; *Engaged*, 1881; *On Bail*, 1881; *Patience*, 1882; *Iolanthe*, 1883; the *Brigands*, 1884; *Princess Ida*, 1884; *Foggerty's Fairy*; *Comedy and Tragedy*, 1884; the *Mikado*, 1885; *An Old Score*; *Charity*, 1885; *Ruddigore*, 1886; the *Yeomen of the Guard*, 1888; the *Gondoliers*, 1889; the *Mountebanks*, 1892; *Rosencrantz and Guildenstern*, 1893; *Utopia, Limited*, 1893.

but here his efforts have not been quite so successful. He seems to lack the quiet restraint necessary, and knows little between sober, earnest gravity and extravagant farcical ebullition. The 'Ne'er-do-weel' and 'Branting-hame Hall' did not attract. The 'Ne'er-do-weel' was one of the few pieces which have been withdrawn, repaired, and tried again, but without altering the result.

Some years ago there was a pleasant, enjoyable entertainment given at the Gaiety—an amateur pantomime—in which several literary men took part. It is to be wished there were more of these exhibitions. The feature of the whole was the Harlequin, discharged by Gilbert *lui-même*. To this he brought his usual conscientiousness; he had learned all the trips and twirls in the most thorough fashion.

The 'Fairy Comedy' excited interest even in fashionable and *blasé* folk. The design, as the author himself told us, was to treat a supernatural element on everyday principles, as though it were an accepted element in human life. He thus made the situation superhuman, and the characters human. Yet it would seem that under such conditions the spectator is led into thinking that the supernatural elements are almost *de trop* and excrescences, and that with a little extra trouble an ordinary play could have been fashioned out of the same materials. We are invited to imagine that people are wearing magic cloaks invisible to the naked eye. The audience is pre-

sumed to believe that persons who are walking about
in the flesh are really invisible or visible, as the occasion
requires. This is really immaterial, considering the
many illusions of the stage, and is rather a strain on
dramatic credulity.

The public is always ready to welcome anything truly
poetical, or that will lift it above the common prosaic
level of life. The 'Fairy Comedy,' his own device,
and, perhaps, his own invention, at once attracted,
though the legend was familiar, and it was curious to
find the ordinary audience listening with pleasure and
even delight to unpretending blank verse conceits and
metaphors of an antique and classical pattern. This
success is greater testimony to Gilbert's ability than
even his later efforts, which were more artfully
adapted to the measure of public taste. There was a
fanciful grace in these formal productions which was
certainly attractive, and Buckstone, now grown old and
deaf and *passé*, contributed not a little as the 'art critic'
to the success of the whole. How 'winsome' was Mrs.
Kendal in her part—what a piquant stateliness did she
exhibit! At this time she and her husband were in the
full bloom of youth and spirit. They were an attractive
pair. There was a series of these fairy tales, which
served their purpose; when it was found that the public
had had enough, the adroit author turned his efforts
in another direction.

To thoroughly appreciate the work that Gilbert and
his coadjutor have done it is only necessary to look
back to the dreary type of 'entertainment'—'Heaven
save the mark!'—that was in favour when they first
began to write. There was then a regular recipe for
these things: given the name and subject, we could
almost forecast beforehand how it would be treated. The
story was a sort of frame or 'clothes-horse' on which to
hang grotesque pantomime dresses, combined with antics
of all kinds, 'breakdown' dances, an infinite amount of
clowning, and what were called topical songs. Whether
it was 'Joan of Arc,' the 'Field of the Cloth of Gold,'
or 'Aladdin,' the same treatment was always adopted.
The chief male characters were taken by females; 'the
prince' or hero was a young woman in trunks and hose;
while the duenna or termagant matron was played by
the low comedian. Stories were often chosen that were
unfamiliar and unsuited. Thus in one a 'Prince of
Burgundy' was brought on whom the pit and galleries
had never heard of, and who, to prove who he was, exhibited on his cuirass a painted bottle and two glasses
filled with very red wine. But indeed a general un-
intelligibility reigned; it was difficult to know 'what it
was all about.' Scenes and antics followed each other;
song followed song in dreary monotony. True, we heard
laughter; but laughter is not an unerring sign of enjoyment. How many dreary, weary hours had we to lay

to the account of what was called so complimentarily 'a
capital burlesque'; or, to quote the hoardings, 'Tir'em-
out's last uproarious burlesque; 400th night.' In those
days we used to read in the newspapers announcements
like the following:

ROYAL THAMES THEATRE.

GLORIOUS AND UNEQUIVOCAL SUCCESS!

CHARLES THE FIRST; or, THE ROYAL *BLOCK*-HEAD.

THE GREAT TOPICAL SONG.
Encored six times every evening.

MISS POLLY BUXOM as KING CHARLES.

MR. D. JACKS as OLD NOLL.

A HOUSE OF COMMONS DEBATE.
THE SPEAKER . . MISS NELLY GRACE.

TAKE THAT BAUBLE AWAY!'
Encored six times nightly.

Take that bauble away,
  Sell it, change it, or spout it;
But here it no longer shall stay—
  No more bones, if you please, about it

DOUBLE BREAKDOWN.

ROYAL THAMES THEATRE.

This was no exaggeration of the modern fashion of putting a bill of fare before a childish public. We were enticed in, entering with a certain alacrity, believing that a delightful night was before us, yet not without misgivings.

Every subject has its serious and its comic side; or, at least, may be so handled as to have its comic side. The lowest manner of producing the last effect is by dress or distortion of face. A man comes on in an absurd costume, and the surprise to the eye produces a laugh. A large nose in a pantomime makes the children scream with enjoyment. But see the dress or large nose a second time and the effect is gone; nay, rather, there is produced a sense of weariness and depression. There was something comic in the Ethiopian serenaders when they first appeared; now no one smiles at their high linen collars and blackened faces. What is wanting is the intellectual element, an underlying earnestness which shall introduce quite a new element. Thus, could we suppose Mr. Huxley—and we ask his pardon for such a supposition—to be so eager, in justification of the negroes and of their state, as to come forward and identify himself with their cause by lecturing in the popular Ethiopian dress—triangular linen, blackened face, woolly hair, &c. —and were he to impress his views earnestly, argumentatively, and passionately, the effect would be irresistibly ludicrous, especially as he grew more earnest and more passionate. The fun would be inexhaustible and ever fresh. This example reveals one of the secrets of true burlesque—an unconsciousness that it is burlesque.

Everyone remembers that exquisite bit of fooling, the 'Rejected Addresses'; and a criticism, made on the imitation of Crabbe, really touched the true key-note of burlesque. It was said that if this poet had been set to write a poem on the fire at Drury Lane, he would have written it much in the same style as the caricaturist had done. Here is the real humour of the thing; the hypothesis of the poet in this new attitude, and his belief that he was as dignified as before. So at an electro-biological séance—to come lower down—the sight of some grave professor dancing away or singing is really ludicrous.

The simple result of all this was repetition, monotony, and fatigue. The screaming new burlesque at the Royal Thames was the screaming old one of six years before, with the cards shuffled. The rival 'Nellys' and 'Pollys' in the pink satin or blue satin 'tights' go through their little dances as before, and 'Mr. D. Jacks' only wears a higher false forehead and a more startling shape of moustache, say five inches longer than his last pair. The 'great topical song' was usually some doggerel of this kind :

> Once more has Rachel been refused
>   To be let out on bail ;
> Enough to make the ladies all
>   Become so very pale.
>
>   *Burden, to a facetious air.*
>   What it means—
>   What it screens—
>   I'm sure I cannot tell.

The ' encoring ten times ' was contrived by the performer retiring at the end of each verse, as if he had quite finished, and reappearing, as if much to his own annoyance. This took in the simple stranger at first ; but more amazing still was it to hear the frantic applause with which rhyme and sentiment far inferior to the above were welcomed. At one of our leading funny theatres a perfect hurricane of applause used to greet something worse than the following extract from ' the great topical song ' :

> And so the cabman's fare, at last,
>   Is settled, nearly quite ;
> I'm sure there's no one here will grudge
>   Poor Cabby all that's right.
>
>   *Burden.*   What it means—
>   What it screens—
>   I'm sure I cannot tell.

Though the old form of burlesque has passed away, being utterly extinguished by the new, we have still with us a sort of kindred entertainment, supported by the untiring Arthur Roberts and his fellows male and female. But this does not profess to be burlesque, it is merely a ' variety ' show, an incoherent collection of songs, jokes, and dances, strung together ' anyhow and everyhow.' This is simply an exhibition, and there are numbers to whom it gives pleasure. But it makes no claim to intellectual entertainment, which is the foundation of all enjoyment. For what appeals merely to the eye and ear, or to the sense of verbal pleasantries, is not merely the lowest form of pleasure, but it is speedily exhausted and becomes monotonous.

In this disastrous state of things there was the fairest opening for anyone possessed of real talent, and Mr. W. S. Gilbert came upon the scene. No one could be better equipped for a public entertainer. For such an office versatility and variety of gifts are almost essential. The fancy and imagination are perpetually at play, new ideas and fresh treatment must be ready at call, otherwise there is repetition and monotony. It is soon found out that the old ideas are being *réchauff’ed*. His experiments in the choice of profession must have furnished him with piquant experiences. Now in a Government office, now a barrister, now a militia captain, he must have seen and learnt a good deal of character and social humours. In his most effective piece we are sure to find some members of the Services, civil, naval or military. Finally, the attraction of the stage became irresistible, though it was not until he was past thirty that he devoted himself formally to dramatic composition.

Full as he was of his ideas of reform, it was natural that at first he should find himself compelled to follow the existing models of burlesque, and almost his earliest piece, 'Dulcamara,' produced at the St. James's Theatre in 1866, was somewhat after the existing pattern, but with a great deal of the more legitimate spirit of burlesque. It was followed by 'Robert the Devil,' which was much after the fashion of Mr. Planché's elegant though really dull burlesques, and which was full of neat responses and pleasant quips.[1] But a production that more closely anticipated his *genre* was 'La Vivandière,' produced in 1868, some seven years before the 'Trial by Jury.' It was given at the defunct Queen's Theatre in Long Acre, erst 'Hullah's Concert Hall.' Brough and Toole and Miss Hodson performed in it, and some of the passages might have found a place in the later Savoy works. Here is a specimen of the fashion in which he

[1] At the time I was dramatic critic to the *Observer*, and having a strong prejudice against all existing forms of burlesque, I inveighed with some severity against this treatment of the subject by Gilbert. I remember receiving from the author a very vehement expostulation and defence, filling, I suppose, a score of folio pages, in which he defended his work with much spirit, and, I think, success. He insisted that he was trying to bring about reform, and was aiming at a higher ideal than then existed. I long preserved this interesting paper, but at the moment I cannot find it.

worked the 'Gilbertian' topic of the English traveller 'turning up his nose' at everything he sees abroad. Lord Margate is addressing some companions at the Grands Mulets on Mont Blanc:

> You all remember, when we left the shore
> Of Rule Britannia, we in concert swore
> We'd do our best on reaching these localities
> To show our undisputed nationalities,
> To show contempt in everything that we did :
> Tell me, my comrades, how have we succeeded?

MARQUIS OF CRANBOURNE ALLEY. I've sworn at all who've hindered my researches.

LORD PENTONVILLE. I've worn my hat in all the foreign churches.

LORD PECKHAM. On all their buildings I've passed verbal strictures,
And poked my walking-stick through all their pictures.
I only carry it about for that use.

MARQUIS OF CRANBOURNE ALLEY. I've decorated all their public statues.

LORD PENTONVILLE. When Frenchmen have conversed with me or you,
We've always turned the talk to Waterloo.

LORD MARGATE. I've half a dozen Frenchmen tried to teach
That I'm twelve times as brave and strong as each,
And showed that this corollary must follow, ,
One Englishman can thrash twelve Frenchmen hollow.
In fact, my friends, wherever we have placed ourselves,
I may say we have thoroughly disgraced ourselves.

Some of these merry conceits might have been found in 'Utopia, Limited.'

Perhaps the nearest approach to the 'Gilbertian humour,' [1] which it certainly anticipated, is to be found in Lewis Carroll's children's books, 'Alice in Wonderland' and 'Through the Looking-glass.' For here was the same system of treatment applied to fairy or nursery tales, the same sincerity in dealing gravely with combinations only found in dreams and nightmares, the same grotesque oddities, which we are yet inclined to accept from the coherence with which they are treated.

The principle of common burlesque, as we have shown, is to take some natural and accepted story and torture it into wildly grotesque shapes. Gilbert and Lewis Carroll adopted an opposite principle—viz. to fashion an eccentric, super-earthly story into shape, and deal with it coherently and logically, so as to compel our sympathies. Of the two methods it is easy to see which has the most art.

. Perhaps a suggestion of Gilbert's efforts is to be found in the 'Bab Ballads,' humorous sketches which he later developed into something more serious and pretentious. This process is indeed significant of his cleverness : all through he has shown this deliberation and

[1] 'I have no notion,' our author writes to me, 'what Gilbertian humour may be. It seems to me that all humour, properly so called, is based upon a grave and quasi-respectful treatment of the ridiculous and absurd.' Notwithstanding this protest, it will be admitted, I think, that there *is* a sort of 'Gilbertian humour' of which the author has the patent.

absence of waste, this putting of his wares to the very best profit. Most remarkable, too, is the persevering fashion in which he has actually taught his public to appreciate him—an absolutely necessary process, for *à priori* it would have been assumed that the conceits of the ' Bab Ballads,' however expanded or dilated, could hardly have been robust enough for the stage. He has even compelled the public to accept and relish conceits of the slightest kind.

The curious grotesque inversion of all things below, which is the note of our author's later work, has always been an essential part of his humour. In the old ' Bab Ballad' days he set down, in ' My Dream,' his quaint notions of what he has called ' Topsy-Turvey-dom ':

> Where babies, much to their surprise,
> Are born astonishingly wise ;
> With every Science on their lips,
> And Art at all their finger-tips.
>
> For, as their nurses dandle them
> They crow binomial theorem,
> With views (it seems absurd to us)
> On differential calculus.
>
> But though a babe, as I have said,
> Is born with learning in his head,
> He must forget it, if he can,
> Before he calls himself a man.

Policemen march all folks away
Who practise virtue every day—
Of course, I mean to say, you know,
What we call virtue here below.

For only scoundrels dare to do
What we consider just and true,
And only good men do, in fact,
What we should think a dirty act.

But strangest of these social twirls,
The girls are boys—the boys are girls!
The men are women, too—but then,
Per contra, women all are men.

With them, as surely as can be,
A sailor should be sick at sea,
And not a passenger may sail
Who cannot smoke right through a gale.

A soldier (save by rarest luck)
Is always shot for showing pluck
(That is, if others can be found
With pluck enough to fire a round).

'How strange!' I said to one I saw
'You quite upset our every law.
However can you get along
So systematically wrong?'

About this time there was in London, beginning
to attract notice, a young musician of great promise,
whose early work had been received with much encouragement. This was Arthur Sullivan, who had been

a choir-boy in the Chapel Royal, and, after studying under Sterndale Bennett, had been sent to Leipsic to complete his musical education. His compositions,

SIR ARTHUR SULLIVAN

such as the 'Tempest' music, were found to exhibit a spontaneity and freedom which offered a contrast to the generally conventional strains of the British

c

musician of the day. Unfortunately for the development of his talent he was attracted by the forms of oratorio, usually written for some great festival, whose rather stilted academical style often checks all airiness and spontaneousness. An experiment, however, which he made in 1876 showed what a vein of buoyant, humorous melody he possessed. Burnand had fashioned the old farce of 'Box and Cox' into a sort of operetta under the title of 'Cox and Box,' and this the young composer set in very delightful fashion, in a sort of joyous Cimarosa vein. Nothing could be more flowing or exhilarating, and it may have suggested to the composer and his future partner a new method of entertaining the public. Burnand has related the almost accident which led to this co-operation. A little piece was wanted for an entertainment at a private house, and, chancing to meet Sullivan, he suggested to him that they should join their talents in turning this little piece into an operetta. I believe the whole was dashed off by both parties in little more than a week's time. Indeed, it was all but 'on the cards,' as it is called, that the composer might have joined his fortunes with this writer, and thus the public might have been destined to laugh over the quips and conceits of the author of 'Happy Thoughts.' This pleasant adaptation of the well-known Buckstonian farce certainly contains some of the most spirited, flowing music the composer ever wrote.

It is quite in the spontaneous vein of the later 'Trial by Jury.' Some of the sentimental strains of this work, such as the aria addressed to the mutton chop, the lullaby, &c., are in the best vein, and surprising in one so young. Another work due to this association was the 'Contrabandista,' said to have been equally brilliant.[1]

Just before the English comedy opera was started the composer was seeking a libretto of an 'eccentric' kind, and applied to his friend, who could only furnish a slight sketch, which was later fashioned into a sort of drawing-room Christmas piece, and fitted with Sullivan's music. Later, the directors of the company proposed that 'F. C. B.' and Cellier should supply an opera, and the plot and some of the 'lines' were prepared; but the scheme fell through. But other influences were now slowly working, and drawing Gilbert and Sullivan into intimate association.

The little elegant dramas presented by the German Reeds (formerly at the Gallery of Illustration), and which have become now a standing London recreation, have been smiled at as though of a 'goody-goody' order, and as providing a harmless, pleasing sort of show, to which a worthy 'Dr. Daly' from the country or strictest matron can bring their children without fear of damage. These pieces deserve higher praise than

---

[1] Some time ago it was proposed to bring forward the *Contrabandista* again (the second act to be re-written).

this, for they were neatly constructed, got up with extraordinary care and finish, and acted with much spirit and emphasis. It is always a happy gift, however, to look for and find what is 'good in everything,' and not to be led, or misled as so many are, by mere forms and surroundings. The ever-ready disdainful 'Pooh-pooh' is fatal to real enjoyment. 'I see nothing to laugh at, said the philosopher 'Pooh-Bah.' 'It is very painful to me to have to say, "How de do, how de do, little girls?" to young persons. I am not in the habit of saying, "How de do, how de do, little girls?" to anybody under the rank of a stockbroker.

> It's hard on us,
> It's hard on us,
> To our prerogative we cling ;
> So pardon us,
> So pardon us,
> If we decline to laugh and sing.'

The German Reed drama anticipated a little the Savoy opera. The music was subsidiary to the words, and was meant to furnish colour and expression. Gilbert once or twice catered for the place, and supplied that very pleasing drama, 'Ages Ago,' with its gracefully managed supernatural element, the living picture-gallery, which he afterwards expanded in 'Ruddigore.' It gave pleasure to many, and a satisfactory proof of its merit is that after so many years its incidents linger in the memory. This sort of chamber drama is really only going back to the original condition of the stage, where intellectual expression is sought under the most favourable conditions, and where play of feature, tone of voice, emphasis, and, above all, intelligent utterance are aimed at. Under the modern conditions of scenic development, blaze of light and colour, these essential elements have become secondary matters. It is sometimes refreshing to find oneself in a small theatre, where the canon strictly obtains that the play, and the play only, is 'the thing.'

There is in Dean Street, Soho, a little theatre, erst 'Miss Kelly's,' a quaint structure built in the garden attached to an old Georgian dwelling. It was at that time unaltered, and the visitors still ascend the old-fashioned stone staircase and pass through the floridly decorated drawing-rooms to get to their places. Miss Selina Dolaro, a sympathetic singer, was then playing in the 'Perichole,' with an odd 'show' or entertainment, described by a cabalistic word of inordinate length. This attraction flagging, she prudently determined to supplement the bill by what was described as 'a new and original cantata called "Trial by Jury,"' which was announced in an unassuming way for the night of March 25, 1875, close on nineteen years ago. Much—according to the familiar phrase—has taken place since then.

The rather unpretending venture was under the direction of D'Oyly Carte, of whom little then was known save that he was a capable and pushing manager. He it was who saw the original merit of the new operetta. I still recall the surprise and hearty approbation with which the little piece was welcomed.

Nothing could be more sprightly or airy than the fashion in which this truly whimsical work was conceived. Each character seemed irresponsible; the miniature theatre and stage were eminently favourable to the effect of the little piece, and every word was heard. The judge was 'Fred' Sullivan, brother of the composer, who had a pleasant humour of his own; Walter Fisher, a lively tenor, long forgotten, was the faithless Lothario; one Hollingsworth the counsel, and Pepper the usher— and 'a good usher too'—the more satisfactory because so unobtrusive; while the winsome Nelly Bromley was the plaintiff, which she gave with unexpected spirit.[1] The reception of this brilliant and witty little satire was of the most hearty kind; there was surprise mingled with the enjoyment, the subject was handled with so light and airy a touch. As was justly remarked, the Law Courts had been often satirised, but never in so whimsical

---

[1] This lady has since left the stage, and is now Mrs. Stuart Wortley. She was associated with a small piece of my own, to which she gave her best energies, and I could not but be struck by her unflagging good-humour and hearty zeal.

and original a fashion. The music, too, was not merely grotesque, but picturesque and dramatic.[1]

First produced on Thursday, March 25, 1875, at the Royalty Theatre

TRIAL BY JURY

AN ORIGINAL DRAMATIC CANTATA

BY

ARTHUR SULLIVAN AND W. S. GILBERT

Dramatis Personæ

THE LEARNED JUDGE	MR. F. SULLIVAN
THE PLAINTIFF	MISS NELLY BROMLEY
THE DEFENDANT	MR. WALTER FISHER
COUNSEL FOR THE PLAINTIFF	MR. HOLLINGSWORTH
USHER	MR. PEPPER
FOREMAN OF THE JURY	
ASSOCIATE	
FIRST BRIDESMAID	

Chorus of Jurymen, &c.

The now popular and facetious Penley filled the humble rôle of ' Foreman of the Jury.'

Of all our authors' joint works I should be inclined to say that this, their first really successful experiment, was the most brilliant, owing to the ease and spontaneousness and unfettered natural humour that pervaded it. It is a trifle, but an admirable trifle, thrown off by both

---

[1] The best and most effective parody of a trial at law is surely Dickens's account of the action against Mr. Pickwick for breach of promise. I have often thought that this might be an effective subject for Sullivan's treatment.

in a moment of exuberant fun, and with little thought of responsibility. The subject, it was felt, lent itself to humorous treatment and to their particular style. It was really delightful to hie to the little theatre and find there an hour's genuine entertainment. It was set forth without pretentious scenery and dresses, and entirely depended on the humorous treatment of the situations. The farcical exaggeration of the incidents of a trial for breach of promise was kept within probable limits, and the whole was enlivened by some original devices. Nothing could be more pleasant than the contrasts between the romantic character of the bride-plaintiff, her faithless swain, the grotesque humours of the judge, the jury, and officers of the court. The composer, too, took care to emphasise the same contrast, allotting charmingly graceful music to plaintiff and defendant, and classically humorous strains to the judge, jury, and officers of the court. The counsel's speech with its persuasive motive is charming, the judge's little autobiography wonderfully comic. I always thought that one of the best passages of the whole, though the least pretentious, was the usher's solemn proclamation:

> Now, jurymen, hear my advice—
> All kinds of vulgar prejudice
>   I pray you set aside:
> With stern judicial frame of mind,
> From bias free of every kind,
>   This trial must be tried!

CHORUS

From bias free of every kind,
   This trial must be tried

USHER

Oh, listen to the plaintiff's case :
Observe the features of her face—
   The broken-hearted bride.
Condole with her distress of mind
From bias free of every kind,
   This trial must be tried!

CHORUS

From bias free, &c.

USHER

And when amid the plaintiff's shrieks,
The ruffianly defendant speaks—
   Upon the other side ;
What *he* may say you needn't mind—
From bias free of every kind,
   This trial must be tried!

CHORUS

From bias free, &c.

The music to which this was wedded had an assumed
dignity and state, with an almost Handelian tone. The
usher's plea for strictest impartiality, all the time dwelling on the charms of the plaintiff, is legitimate humour
of the best kind.

Here was first introduced that Gilbert-Sullivan recipe
of making some dignified personage—a judge or 'Lord
High' something—supply a humorous biography of him-

self, and in many verses ; a duty which later usually fell to the facetious Grossmith. It may not be strictly legitimate that a personage should thus explain *au grand sérieux* all his methods, as though he were actually conscious of his own absurdity. The practice was steadily adhered to for many years and in many pieces.

Dickens had his grotesque Mr. Justice Stareleigh in 'Pickwick'; but Gilbert's judge was a different character altogether. His entry is heralded by the uprising of the jury, who acclaim him, as it were, in a fine stately strain:

> All hail, great judge !
> To your *bright rays*
> We never grudge
> Ecstatic praise.
>
> May each decree
> As statute rank,
> And never be
> Reversed in Banc.

The judge graciously answers in recitative :—

> For these kind words accept my thanks, I pray,
> A breach of promise we've to try to-day.
> But firstly, if the time you'll not begrudge,
> I'll tell you how I came to be a judge.
> ALL. He'll tell us how he came to be a judge !

The dramatic compression of these lines and the pleasantly abrupt transition, 'But firstly,' &c., is the best and most legitimate vein of humour.

Song—Judge

When I, good friends, was called to the Bar,
    I'd an appetite fresh and hearty,
But I was, as many young barristers are,
    An impecunious party.
I'd a swallow-tail coat of a beautiful blue—
    A brief which I bought of a booby—
A couple of shirts and a collar or two,
    And a ring that looked like a ruby!

Chorus repeats, ' A couple of shirts,' &c. This sort of grotesque repetition is one of our author's happiest devices (see also the Police Chorus).

Judge

In Westminster Hall I danced a dance,
    Like a semi-despondent fury;
For I thought I should never hit on a chance
    Of addressing a British jury—
But I soon got tired of third-class journeys,
    And dinners of bread and water;
So I fell in love with a rich attorney's
    Elderly, ugly daughter.

The rich attorney, he jumped with joy,
    And replied to my fond professions:
' You shall reap the reward of your pluck, my boy,
    At the Bailey and Middlesex Sessions.
You'll soon get used to her looks,' said he,
    ' And a very nice girl you'll find her!
She may very well pass for forty-three
    In the dusk, with a light behind her!'

At length I became as rich as the Gurneys—
　An incubus then I thought her,
So I threw over that rich attorney's
　Elderly, ugly daughter.
The rich attorney my character high
　Tried vainly to disparage—
And now, if you please, I'm ready to try
　This breach of promise of marriage !

CHORUS

And now, if you please, &c.

JUDGE. For now I'm a judge !
ALL. And a good judge too !
JUDGE. Yes, now I'm a judge !
ALL. And a good judge too !

JUDGE

Though all my law is fudge,
Yet I'll never, never budge,
But I'll live and die a judge !

As a composition this song is admirable, the 'points' being shortly touched and made as effective as possible. It was sung by every *buffo* of private life in hundreds of drawing-rooms. Some of its phrases have become stock quotations, such as 'In the dusk, with a light behind her'; 'elderly, ugly daughter,' &c.

The entry of the plaintiff with her bridesmaids in a sort of dance is accompanied by the most attractive music; indeed, nothing is more captivating than the different changes of style and tone which are suited to each situation. The sympathies of judge and jury are

at once enlisted, the latter giving vent to their feelings in
the plaintive strain, 'Comes the broken flower,' &c., the
judge exclaiming:

> *O never since I joined the human race*
> Saw I so exquisite a face.
> THE JURY (*shaking their finger at him*). Ah! sly dog!
> Ah! sly dog!
> JUDGE. Now, say you, is she not designed for capture?
> JURY. We've but one word, my Lud, and that is 'rapture.'
> PLAINTIFF (*curtseying*). Your kindness quite overpowers.
> JURY. We love you fondly, and would make you ours.

This, too, is dramatically excellent. Then the counsel begins his speech, in a persuasive air, somewhat in
the shape of the eternal 'Last Rose of Summer':

> With a sense of deep emotion
> I approach this painful case,
> For I never had a notion
> That a man could be so base,
> Or deceive a girl confiding,
> Vows, *et cetera*, deriding.

How real the agitation of the enticing plaintiff, who,
about to give her evidence, makes as though she would
faint! 'That she is reeling,' the judge says, 'is plain
to me.' And the jury, to her, 'If faint you're feeling,
lean on me!' She falls sobbing on the foreman's
breast, and feebly murmurs:

> I shall recover
> If left alone.

> JURY. O, perjured monster,
>   Atone! Atone!
> FOREMAN. Just like a father
>   I wish to be.
>   O, if you'd rather,
>   Lean on me.

This competition of attentions between judge and jury is truly grotesque.

She finally reclines on the judge, and her counsel says:

> Fetch some water
> From far Cologne.
> ALL. For the sad slaughter,
>   Atone! Atone!

Then they burst into tragic denunciation:

> Monster, monster, dread our fury,
> There's the judge, and we're the jury.

Altogether, a happy parody of the methods of grand opera. The *finale* is not so good, and becomes a sort of general romp.[1]

It was in this piece that the author first made use of a happy device which he afterwards largely developed. His object was to avoid the conventional methods of using the chorus, nearly always a professional crowd who came in at intervals and raised their voices. A

---

[1] The length of these and future extracts from these pleasant pieces will, I think, not be objected to, as they will bring back to the reader many pleasant moments enjoyed while making his Savoy education.

more probable and natural method occurred to him. Assuming that the conspicuous personages must have some following connected with or dependent on them, he contrived to emphasise these attendants in a picturesque way. They had the air not of a 'crowd,' but of a large number of friends. Thus in 'Trial by Jury' the brides-maids and the jury raised their voices. In the 'Pina-fore' the famous 'sisters, cousins, and aunts of the First Lord' were the chorus. In other pieces he would have a number of officers, or some policemen. There were also the 'House of Lords'; and the 'ancestors' in 'Ruddigore.' It is astonishing what a variety of groups of this kind our author managed to devise out of his teeming imagination. The chorus thus became a personage, not merely a collection of voices introduced to swell the music. With the view of individualising it as much as possible he generally made a few members prominent, and thus is brought to our recollection many out of those charming groups of girls who lent such an attraction to his pieces.

About the year 1876 there was formed a society called the English Comic Opera Company, which had secured the Opera Comique for its performances. Their secretary and adviser was the manager of the Royalty, D'Oyly Carte, a man of much tact and sound business instincts— a born manager, in fact. This is proved by his showing himself 'equal to either fortune.' He has known how to

secure success, and, what is more difficult, to retain it.
No one but a man of ability could have extricated him-

MR. D'OYLY CARTE
(*From a Photograph by Walery, Regent Street*)

self from the tremendous failure of the ambitious and
costly venture in Shaftesbury Avenue.[1]

[1] 'The Comedy-Opera Company was entirely Mr. Carte's idea, and
his own creation. He was manager at the Royalty at the time of
the original production of *Trial by Jury*, and after that piece he always

D'Oyly Carte, the creator and present manager of the Savoy Theatre, was the son of Richard Carte, a name known to all flute-players, and a partner in the firm of Rudall & Carte. After leaving the London University he followed musical agency as a profession, and among other enterprises directed Mario's ' Farewell Tour.' But about 1876 he began to work out his great scheme of an English Comic Opera Company, and was adroit enough to see what advantages he would gain by securing the aid of that clever pair, Gilbert and Sullivan. It might have been said to him, as one of the characters does to the Pirate King in the ' Penzance ' operetta : ' You mean to develop comic opera into a system by the aid of new talent, and look to having a special home for it in a new, specially devised, and attractive theatre, made brilliant by the introduction of electric lighting ? ' And the answer may have been a dry, ' *Yes, that is the idea.*' This was an almost gigantic plan, which at that time must have appeared quite utopian ; but he was encouraged by the aid of his efficient wife, one of the best ' women of business ' of the day. This was Miss Cowper-Black, or ' Lenoir,' a name she later as-

had the idea of getting Mr. Gilbert and Sir Arthur Sullivan to write a larger work together ; but it was a long time before he could get this arranged, and before they were both ready and able to undertake it, and then a theatre had to be found, and the money got together to start it. The Comedy-Opera Company came to an end after the production of *Pinafore.'*—*Letter from Mrs. D'Oyly Carte.*

D

sumed. After a brilliant career at the London University she took up stage business and management, for which she had a marked taste, and became translator and secretary to the Opera Comique Company. In a few months she had completely made herself mistress of the system. She crossed the Atlantic about fifteen times, and at one period was directing four travelling companies. She combined with these arduous duties the agency for lectures, and arranged and directed the tours of Archibald Forbes, Matthew Arnold, Oscar Wilde, and the now almost forgotten Sergeant Ballantine. It is not 'generally known' that the great Savoy Hotel was another venture of this enterprising pair, and Mrs. D'Oyly Carte is said to have settled all the details of the vast scheme.

When the enterprising partners—or trio, rather—were entering on their new operatic venture, they were met by the grave difficulty of finding suitable interpreters for their work. There were plenty of the old well-trained singers; but these were formed to the old methods. They cast about for young and promising talent which they could mould to their own fashion. This system has been found to work admirably at the Savoy, which has since become a large and regular school where young persons of promise and ability are certain to find an opening for their abilities. Freshness and novelty are thus secured. All that is required is a good voice and musical taste, with a certain natural enthusiasm; the instructions of the librettist and the *genius loci* do the rest.

MR. GEORGE GROSSMITH

At this time there was a brilliant and promising young man named George Grossmith, who was what is called an 'entertainer,' and had the fairest prospects of success in this way. He was highly popular for his

spirits and fun, and overflowing with humorous conceits and devices, which found expression in songs
and recitations, little comedies and scenes, which he
presented in so vivid a fashion and with so many resources of expression as to have the effect of a drama;
from his finish and certainty he seems to have been the
most perfect of the many 'delineators' who have
attempted this attractive fashion of entertaining. He
was an excellent musician, for whom his pianoforte was
almost an instinctive form of expression, like the human
voice. He had performed on the stage occasionally,
and had once or twice attempted such parts as Paul
Pry.

One night in November 1877 he was asked by
Mr. Arthur Sullivan to return with him to his rooms in
Victoria Street, where in the company of a number of
choice spirits a pleasant evening was passed. The
stranger or 'new man' cheerfully contributed his little
talents; everyone went away pleased with him. George
Grossmith is indeed good company: his anecdotes,
told unaffectedly and without effort or artifice, fall into
dramatic shape, and seem to be a portion of his entertainment. They are set off by the most expressive of
faces. His tales, too, are not of the kind that actors tell,
half professional, and turning on some comic speech or
incident, but deal with grotesqueness of character, or
some oddity of social life. He is a most acute observer

of such things, and sees humour and humorous situations which would escape others less trained.

In a few days he received an unexpected proposal from the composer, offering him a part in a new piece, which it was thought he would play admirably. He was delighted and yet undecided, for this involved abandoning his own proper profession. If he failed—or rather, if he did not succeed—it would be impossible for him to return ; for his correct and serious clients who welcomed him at their lecture-rooms would not accept him after he had been on ' the wicked stage.' His father and some of his friends were against the step. So, too, were the directors of the Comedy-Opera Company (Limited), who thought it imprudent to take an untried ' hand.' Even the adventurous D'Oyly Carte was cold or scarcely encouraging.[1] The engagement, however, was at last settled. When he was going over the part with Gilbert, he hazarded the objection, ' For the part of a magician, I thought you required a fine man with a large voice.' I can still see Gilbert's humorous expression as he replied, ' No, that's just what we *don't* want ! '—a light touch

[1] In the discussion on the amount of salary, Grossmith held out for an increase of three guineas. The manager asked him to lunch, to talk the matter over. Some admirable Steinberg Cabinet and other delicacies were produced. After the lunch was despatched the salary question was discussed ; but under the agreeable influence of the Steinberg Cabinet three guineas seemed a trivial thing, and Grossmith gave way. 'I calculate,' he used to say, 'that that lunch cost me about 1,800*l*.'

that really involves the whole philosophy of the Gilbertian opera, and shows how much the finesse of its humour was opposed to the common standards.[1]

Another promising recruit was Rutland Barrington, who seems to have been fitted in the most à *propos* way for the interpretation of the new methods of opera. His peculiar tranquil or impassive style has always exactly suited the characters allotted to him, and it would now be difficult to imagine a Savoy opera without him. He alone, I think, has been with it—with one slight interruption—from the beginning to the present moment. He is usually cast for some impossible monarch, prime minister, or personage of 'Lord High' degree, possessed of some fantastic theories which he essays to carry out with supreme gravity; and though his methods and humours have been much the same all through, there is sufficient variety in his intellectual conceptions of each part. We recall with enjoyment his unctuous clergyman, his sea captain in the 'Pinafore,' his various Court functionaries, and his eccentric monarchs. Rarely or never does he pass the limits of a becoming gravity, or become more extravagant than is necessary. He can become delightfully helpless and inefficient, or

---

[1] Grossmith has related his life and adventures in an agreeable little volume, *A Society Clown*, full of good strokes of human character and humour. It shows that he had severe and valuable training (not to say a struggle) for many years—a most profitable and blessed thing for a performer.

break out into exuberance when it is called for. His full tall figure and round face help the effect.

Another of the more valuable members of the corps was the piquant and vivacious Jessie Bond, whose very presence and animated tones seemed to quicken the action the moment she appeared. She enjoyed an extraordinary favour and popularity: audiences seemed glad to see her, to have her before their eyes. She has figured, I believe, in every Savoy opera save the last, and has always been a welcome aid. Another steady pillar of the enterprise, who has been constant to it till this moment, was Rosina Brandram, with her rich contralto, and who is generally cast for some austere duenna. She, like some of the others, owes her training to the entertainment stage.

Grossmith and his career suggest here some reflections which are really connected with the art of stage expression. Many entertainers have been tempted by their successes in this walk to venture on the stage; and it may be an interesting speculation here to inquire to what extent the training of the platform is serviceable for exhibition in the theatre. George Grossmith and Arthur Cecil present two notable examples where the change has been made with success, but it must be said that on the whole the two systems or processes are opposed. Theatrical effects are large, broad, and general, whereas those of the entertainer are minute, and

'stippled in' as it were. The two methods start from
the same point, but seem to recede from each other. The
entertainer has to rely upon the words and on his face and
voice; the actor on his internal conception, using the same
means to express what he feels. When the entertainer
brings his talents to a theatre it is likely enough that
his methods will prove ineffective, and the minute
details—his stock-in-trade—become overpowered. Real
talent, however, will triumph over such a disability, and
secure the artist the necessary 'breadth.' Still, it is
difficult to unlearn; and in most cases the old system, in
which the performer feels he can make his best efforts,
will cling to him. Thus Alfred Bishop, Arthur Cecil,
and Grossmith to this hour show traces of their early
training on the platform rather than on the stage.
Bishop, when performing at the Lyceum as Old
Ashton, showed little of the breadth necessary for so
great an area; and Cecil has abundance of delicate
touches, which, however, become ineffective in a large
theatre. Defects of this kind are scarcely noticeable in
the case of Grossmith, who has only appeared on a stage
where such touches are acceptable and really necessary;
for at the Savoy every word and gesture are calculated
beforehand, and become of importance.

Still, there can be no doubt that this 'entertainer'
element is more and more leavening legitimate stage

performances; and that the present fashion requires the
personal efforts of the actor to be more and more developed is shown by the constant intrusion of the
music-hall performer and his devices, for whom and
for which the public have shown an extraordinary
fancy. The effects of this change will no doubt have by-
and-by an extraordinary influence on the stage. Nor is
it fanciful to say that the development of the manager-
actor system is intimately connected with this change;
for such is really the development of the personal element,
carried as far as it can well go. The system, however,
has its serious disadvantages, for when by some accident
the personal element is withdrawn, the 'show' loses
attraction; which is proved by the instance of Grossmith,
whose retirement was a serious loss to the Savoy.

The entertainment seems almost to have changed
its character, and has taken many shapes. At the
beginning a single versatile person was himself the
whole play, and supplied from his intellectual wallet
characters, dialogue, music—everything. In our time
this grew into the pleasing drawing-room entertainment
given by the German Reeds at the Gallery of Illustration
and St. George's Hall. This school became almost the
nursery of the Savoy opera, and most of its interpreters—Grossmith, Miss Brandram, Mrs. Howard Paul,
Barrington, the Temple Brothers, Arthur Cecil, and

many more—have graduated in this college, and have there happily acquired the art of minute touching and delicate strokes.

The entertainer's art, trivial as it may appear, is really the quintessence of the drama; for in its most orthodox shape it is independent of dresses, scenery, and what is called facial 'make-up.' These things the performer has to supply from his own intellectual 'properties.' With the skilful entertainer before us, holding us with his vivacious eye, making his mobile features express, not imitate, the twists and oddities of character, while he plays on his voice as on an instrument, we are beguiled by his cunning, and fancy that whole tapestries of life are being unrolled before us. This sort of show, therefore, has always enjoyed favour; and the listeners, being in direct contact with their host, naturally feel a partiality or goodwill for the amiable being who, for some two long hours or so, devotes himself to their entertainment. When it is of the first class, nothing gives more genuine pleasure—a pleasure compounded of an admiration of the performer's gifts and of the diverting quips and humours which he displays.

This pastime, as I said, has taken various shapes, being moulded according to the 'form and pressure of the time.' In the last century a leading portion of the actor's equipment was mimicry, and too often mimicry

of his brethren. Dog surely should not eat dog. Even
Garrick descended to this. Foote, a licensed free-lance,
who made a living by taking off public personages in his
comedies and entertainments, was perhaps the greatest
showman of the age, and, from his great powers of wit,
vivacity, recklessness and unscrupulousness, maintained
his hold upon his admirers until his death. Personality
is perhaps the greatest attraction known to the stage.
In our time, happily, it is not tolerated at all, though
many will recall what unbounded enjoyment and interest
were excited by Gilbert's piece which, years ago, drew all
London to the little Court Theatre—the ' Happy Land,'
in which three members of the Government were introduced. But the exhibition, which was not an ill-natured
one, was speedily moderated.

In 1747 Foote arranged an entertainment at the
little Haymarket Theatre called the ' Diversions of the
Morning,' which had extraordinary success ; nearly all
the characters were rude portraits of personages well
known on town. The public rushed to see, but, as he
also performed the regular drama in an unlicensed
theatre, the authorities interfered. He then thought of
a rather colourable device to elude the law : ' Mr. Foote
begs the favour of his friends to come and drink a dish
of chocolate with him ; and he hopes there will be a great
deal of comedy and some joyous spirits ; he will endeavour to make the morning as diverting as possible.

Tickets for this entertainment to be had at St. George's Coffee House, Temple Bar, without which no person will be admitted. N.B.—Sir Dilberry Dibble and Lady Froth have absolutely promised.' It was found impossible to suppress this sort of performance, and Mr. Foote's 'show' became the rage. His plan was to introduce a number of young performers whom he affected to be instructing for the stage, rehearsing with them, and making sarcastic remarks on the leading writers, politicians, &c., of the day.

Foote, who in the way of ridicule spared nobody, seems to have been himself most sensitive and thin-skinned when any liberties were taken with *him*. It is amusing to find that he was to suffer acutely from an obscure parasite whom he himself had instructed in the art—Tate Wilkinson, a forward, clever lad, one of the 'supers' at Drury Lane, who had been exhibited by him on the stage as 'a pupil.' This youth had an extraordinary talent for low mimicry, and was encouraged by his employer to exhibit it. One night at the Dublin Theatre, after giving his imitation of Mrs. Woffington, he was greeted with so much applause that he was on the instant tempted to an imprudent step. 'A sudden thought,' he tells us, 'occurred. I felt all hardy, all alert, all nerve, and immediately advanced six steps: and before I spoke I received the full testimony of true imitation. The master, as he was called, sat on the stage at the same time. I repeated twelve or fourteen lines of the very prologue he had spoken that night, and, before Mr. Foote, presented his own self, his manner, his voice, his oddities, and so exactly hit that the glee and pleasure it gave may be easily conceived to see and hear the mimic mimicked. The suddenness of the action tripped up his audacity so much that he, with all his effrontery, sat foolish, wishing to appear equally pleased with the audience, but knew not how to play that difficult part.' A graphic picture. The jackal became a thorn in the greater mimic's side. He early appropriated the entertainment, and travelled over the kingdom, 'giving Tea' everywhere, and 'taking off,' in his vulgar way, his late master and the leading actors.

After Foote, who had been absurdly called 'the English Aristophanes,' a humorous song-writer named George Alexander Steevens devised a very original species of entertainment. When the curtain rose, or the scene was 'drawn,' the audience saw before them a table with a vast number of heads or busts. The entertainer then came forward and delivered what was called a 'Lecture on Heads'; and, taking one of the specimens in his hand, would illustrate it with a number of satirical observations on politicians, authors, &c. Thus he would begin, 'Here we have the head of a divine,' &c. The lecture 'on Heads' obtained great celebrity, was printed in a volume, passed through many editions, and was thought exquisitely humorous; though, on reading it over now, it seems much laboured, rather jejune, and tedious.

There was a roistering actor, Lee Lewes, who enjoys a sort of fame from his having been selected by Goldsmith to 'create' the part of Young Marlow, a jovial being and a teller of convivial stories, which, when published later in four volumes, read ineptly enough. The dramatic story seemed to be the form then in demand for this kind of entertainment, in which various characters were contrasted, and a dialogue kept up, the whole concluding with some boisterous situation. No doubt the applause of the supper-table suggested the sort of article that would suit a larger audience. One of Lee Lewes's most effective scenes was his account of a dialogue between Garrick and Lord Orrery, on the subject of Mossop the actor. Garrick's vanity, it was known, was so sensitive that it could be played on artfully, and Lord Orrery, for his own and his lady's amusement, would noisily extol the actor's voice to provoke Garrick's dissent; after which the nobleman would abruptly and cordially change his view, and abuse Mossop heartily. Thus he would loudly extol Mossop's voice, and when Garrick hesitated or doubted, the other would declare that 'he roared like a bull.' 'We always called him *Bull-Mossop.*'

Charles Dibdin, Incledon, and other popular singers

also gave 'entertainments.' Incledon, for a time, joined
his talents with those of Mathews, and the pair travelled
about the kingdom together. But the most successful
of these showmen was Bannister, one of Garrick's
'school,' as it was called, and an actor of much reputation. One morning in 1807 he rushed in to George
Colman, carrying a huge bundle of songs, recitations,
humorous stories, &c., which he wished his lively friend
to fashion into an 'entertainment.' Colman had just
planned a week of delicious lethargy and idleness, but
he cheerfully accepted the task, and in a few days had
reduced the mass of inchoate drolleries into form. It
had become 'Bannister's Budget,' which the actor at
once took into the country with extraordinary success.
It appears to have been a medley of detached stories,
songs, recitations, and 'odds and ends' of all kinds.
One item, for instance, was entitled 'Two Ways of
Telling a Story'; the survivor of a shipwreck was supposed to relate all the horrors of the scene in the most
dramatic way, the storm, the roaring of the billows, the
imminent destruction, rescue, &c.; a 'Jack Tar' then
gave *his* account, but in a light, careless, unconcerned
fashion, as though the whole were a joke. There was a
gruesome, grotesque tale of some length called 'The
Superannuated Sexton,' with such characters as Doctors
Doublechops and Lank Jaws. He would also describe
—to great applause—his first introduction, as a youth

aspiring to the stage, to Mr. Garrick.. He found the great man shaving, his chin covered with soapsuds. The actor bade him 'never mind,' but recite a speech from 'Hamlet'—say 'Angels and ministers of grace,' &c. During the recitation Garrick is described as stropping or lathering, or 'taking himself by the nose,' with grotesque effect. At the close 'he turned quick on me, and thrusting his half-shaved face close to mine, exclaimed in a tone of ridicule, "Angels and ministers of grace, *yaw—waw—waw*!" then finished his operation, and putting on his wig, good-naturedly said, "Come, young gentleman, eh? Let us see what we can do," then recited the whole speech in his best style.' Bannister was summoned by the King to give his show at Windsor, and a number of the nobility were invited. He was naturally a little nervous, when the good-humoured Princess Sophia said, to reassure him, 'You are frightened: I declare, if you don't do it well, *I shall hiss you*, Mr. Bannister!'

Our modern peripatetics, who have their shrewd 'agents in advance' to prepare the ground and secure 'dates,' would smile at the careless, unbusinesslike ways of these early pioneers. Bartley, a fellow-actor, used to relate how, when attending one of Bannister's performances at the Rooms in Edinburgh, he was requested, on coming out, by his friend to take up the money from the doorkeepers. He was disappointed to find that the whole sum only came to 90*l*. 'Pooh!' said the easy-going Bannister, 'if I am pleased, why not you?' They met some men on the staircase who, it seems, were stationed at the other entrances, and had 60*l*. more to give them. Bannister declared that but for his friend he would have gone away without it. The results of 'the Budget' were indeed so satisfactory, that though Colman declined remuneration the actor insisted on releasing him from a bond for 700*l*. as a token of his gratitude. It must be said, however, that neither party would have gained or lost by the transaction, as the impecunious Colman, who spent the chief portion of his days within the Rules of the King's Bench, would never have dreamed of repaying it, or any other obligation.

Mathews the Elder was one of the most versatile and accomplished men that have adorned the entertainment. He had a boundless store of devices, his talents for comedy and mimicry contributing much to the gaiety of his generation. In fact, his stores of 'harmless pleasure' were of a marvellous kind. He was a most delightful companion—vivacious, 'incompressible,' like Foote—an affectionate father and husband, while his letters are truly admirable for their liveliness, genuineness, and graphic style. His power of ventriloquism, and of disguising his features and figure—not by

E

mechanical art, but by sheer mental effort—were extraordinary and unusual; witness that 'Mr. Pennyman'
who was perpetually found behind the scenes, plaguing
everybody, though the doorkeepers were on the watch
not to admit him. At table friends would find themselves annoyed by a quarrelsome stranger, who would
appear and disappear in a marvellous and all but supernatural way. It was not surprising that he should have
utilised these gifts for the public diversion and his own
profit. After some slight experiments, in the year 1808
he determined to make the venture, employing James
Smith, one of the authors of the 'Rejected Addresses,'
to furnish him with an entertainment. This was the
first of a long series supplied by the same 'eminent
hand,' who was assisted by Poole, the author of 'Paul
Pry.' The form was usually the same—a journey in a
mail coach or in a diligence—literally a 'vehicle' for
introducing the varied humours of the performer—with
many grotesque or eccentric passages. The 'Mail
Coach' was long popular, the whole of the incidents of
such a journey being humorously described.

An adroit manager—one of that Arnold managerial
family which still holds the Lyceum—had suggested to
him this mode of utilising his talents, and now induced
him to mortgage his services to him for a term of years.
The thoughtless player, dazzled by the prospect of a
fixed income, signed and sealed with a light heart, and

in due course made his appearance at a London theatre. His success was extraordinary; nothing so novel, so exhilarating, had been seen for many a day. The bill set forth 'he will exhibit an entire new entertainment, consisting of songs, recitations, imitations, ventriloquism, entitled "The Mail Coach, or Rambles in Yorkshire." Part I. Recitations, introductory address; general improvement in the conveyance of live lumber as exemplified in the progress of the Heavy Coach, light coach, and mail; whimsical description of an expedition to Brentford. Song, "Mail Coach." Recitation: description of the Passengers; Lisping Lady; Frenchman. Song, "Twenty-four Lord Mayors' Shows." Mr. and Mrs. Nicky Numskull; cross-examination of a Pig. Song, "The Assizes."'

It will be seen from this programme that the shape of these entertainments has been somewhat conserved to our day—alternations of song and speech, more or less formal. Mathews always stood behind a little table, on which were two shaded candles, whilst an accompanyist sat at a piano. He relied almost entirely on his facial expression to produce changes, though he would sometimes hurriedly wrap a handkerchief round his head to simulate an old lady. Later, however, he introduced dresses, and became what is called 'a quick-change artist'—a descent into a lower walk of business. What astonished his audience was the elegance, airiness, and

buoyancy of the whole performance—the variety of
talents displayed.   They would hear a conversation
between *five* different persons—a valet talking with a
child, a butler, the housekeeper, &c.   The success was
immense, the crowds enormous.   But presently the
much-followed performer discovered that he had sold
himself at a deplorably low price.   The bond which he
had so recklessly signed was full of penalties and for-
feitures; he had placed himself, with all his talents,
faculties, and powers, at the disposal of a master.   This,
however, he had done 'with his eyes open'; it was a
speculative transaction, and, had there been failure, the
manager would have been bound.   He was not, however, pitiless, and consented to a liberal revision of
the arrangement.   There were a few rare veteran playgoers—notably the late amiable, genial Fladgate, the
father of the Garrick Club—who could recall Mathews
and his pleasant exhibitions.   It is curious to think
that we had amongst us only yesterday one who had
seen and talked with Kemble and Siddons, and also with
Irving.

After Mathews a change seems to have come over
the style of these entertainments.   During the past
forty or fifty years they have reverted to the old form.
They exhibit more finesse and delicacy, more refinement of character, and are, indeed, addressed to a
superior description of audience.   This is no doubt

owing to the disappearance of the old farce, which seems to have altogether 'gone out.' Much more was required from the impersonator, who found dramatic aid in his piano, at which he sat and over which his fingers strayed, and from which he only occasionally rose. It became for him a second, even more eloquent, voice.

Perhaps the first of these reformers was the inimitable John Parry, who was a comic-song writer rather than an entertainer, and he seems to have adopted this mode of exhibition with a view of introducing his songs to notice. These were sung in private circles by amateur humourists and had a large sale. A good specimen of his style was the well-known 'Wanted, a Governess':

> Wanted, a governess, fitted to fill
> The post of tuition with competent skill,
> In a gentleman's family, highly genteel,
> Where 'tis hoped that the lady will try to conceal
> Any fanciful airs or fears she may feel
> In this gentleman's family, highly genteel.

Each verse wound up with an accompanying 'crash' on the piano to the words '*Wanted*, a governess!' This was then thought exquisitely frolicsome!

Another of these exhibiting song-writers and singers still lives—the author of the 'Ship on Fire' and 'Cheer, boys, cheer,' and who, some forty years ago,

was admired and talked of, and, in the provinces
particularly, drew large houses. This is Henry
Russell. His songs, however, were the *pièce de résistance*,
and people came to hear the songs and join in the
choruses. They were linked together by a mildly
humorous commentary, chiefly personal or anecdotal,
as when, after giving vent in his richly mellifluous and
deliberate tones to the once popular lines,

> Woodman, spare that tree,
>   Touch not a single bough ;
> In youth it sheltered me ;
>   And I'll protect it now !

he would proceed to relate ' a little anecdote '—how, at
some house, a gentleman, standing up among the
audience, earnestly asked him, ' Mr. Russell ! Mr.
Russell ! *Was* the tree spared ? '

Albert Smith's ' Ascent of Mont Blanc ' was for some
years a standing attraction at the Egyptian Hall, but
this was somewhat panoramic. The agreeable Albert
told the story in a lively fashion, and, according to his
mood, would vary it with extemporised humorous passages. Sometimes, recognising a friend in the audience, he would allude to him by name, fathering on
him some jest or speech—to the embarrassment of the
individual. During the succeeding period there was a
more debased form of the entertainment, the performers

beginning to rely upon dresses, 'quick changes,' and the like, conspicuous professors being Woodin and a diverting, versatile being named Valentine Vox, and Duval. It was natural that the form should take a fresh development, and we presently find two performers giving their attractions in a sort of dialogue. From this to a slight play was but a natural advance, and for a long period—down, indeed, to the present moment— the German Reeds have contributed to increase the general gaiety of the nation. It was here, as we have seen, that Arthur Cecil and Corney Grain learned the measure of their powers in the old school of 'delineation,' though the former speedily passed on to the stage, thus reversing the practice of his predecessors, who passed from the stage to the platform. This modern school was to be further strengthened by the accession of George Grossmith, who, after quitting the platform, became one of the pillars of the Savoy, which he has again recently forsaken to return to the platform; and it is said now that, in spite of large profits, he meditates a return to the more exciting glories of the stage. It would be difficult to say too much of the extraordinary versatility of these performers. Their sketches of society, of its follies and weaknesses, offer a power of intellectual analysis and observation that is remarkable. An anchorite's muscles would relax. They also possess an amazing fertility in their performance on the piano, which, in an informal and unartificial way, is made to illustrate all they say.

Such is the genesis and development of this peculiar form of the drama, and which, there can be no doubt, is deeply seated in the affections of British audiences.

But I have strayed from our Savoy Opera home into a somewhat antiquarian review. Still, the subject is an interesting one, and has, besides, a close connection with the Savoy methods.

The 'Sorcerer'—the first attempt of the Comedy-Opera Company—was of a rather serious and dignified cast. It seemed as though both author and composer were a little fettered by the sense of their office. They were by-and-by to be in a situation of 'more freedom and less responsibility,' and with the happiest effect. They were now feeling their way, as it were. The supernatural element of the piece was accountable for this tone, the composer finding himself compelled, as it were, to treat it with due solemnity and even gravity. The press welcomed it with almost tumultuous praise.[1]

---

[1] Indeed, some journals were so indiscriminate in their approbation as to heartily commend certain 'numbers' which were not performed at all!

*First produced at the Opera Comique, under the management
of the Comedy-Opera Company (Mr. R. D'Oyly Carte,
Manager), November 17, 1877*

THE SORCERER

Dramatis Personæ

SIR MARMADUKE POINTDEXTRE (*an Elderly Baronet*)	MR. RICHARD TEMPLE
ALEXIS (*of the Grenadier Guards—his Son*)	MR. GEORGE BENTHAM
DR. DALY (*Vicar of Ploverleigh*) . . .	MR. RUTLAND BARRINGTON
NOTARY	MR. F. CLIFTON
JOHN WELLINGTON WELLS (*of J. W. Wells & Co., Family Sorcerers*) . . .	MR. GEORGE GROSSMITH
LADY SANGAZURE (*a Lady of Ancient Lineage*)	MRS. HOWARD PAUL
ALINE (*her Daughter—betrothed to Alexis*) .	MISS ALICE MAY
MRS. PARTLET (*a Pew-opener*) . . .	MISS EVERARD
CONSTANCE (*her Daughter*)	MISS GIULIA WARWICK

Chorus of Peasantry

ACT I.—Grounds of Sir Marmaduke's Mansion

(*Half-an-hour is supposed to elapse between Acts I. and II.*)

ACT II.—The same Scene by Moonlight

TIME—THE PRESENT DAY[1]

No one then dreamed that this was to be the opening

---

[1] On its later revival, Mr. Durward Lely took Mr. George Power's part; Miss Brandram, Miss Leonora Braham, Miss A. Dorée, and Miss Jessie Bond the parts of Lady Sangazure, Aline, Mrs. Partlet, and Constance. The opera was revised and partly rewritten for this occasion. The costumes were by MM. Auguste, Caler & Co., J. B. Johnstone, Ede & Son, Frank Smith & Co., Hobson & Co.

of a striking series of successes, and a series that was to be sustained with an unflagging interest for some seventeen years. The chief point of interest was

JOHN WELLINGTON WELLS

THE INCANTATION

how would Grossmith, the new candidate, acquit himself as John Wellington Wells, the traveller in drugs, 'penny curses,' and the rest? The spare and wiry little figure, the small, intelligent face, full of finesse and expression, was at once a success. No one could have received more friendly encouragement. His 'patter song,' as it is called—a number of rhymes uttered with extraordinary rapidity and clearness—enlevéed the house. This was to become an established pattern in a Savoy opera, following the precedent of the judge's little auto-

biography in 'Trial by Jury.' A genuine surprise was in store for the audience when, at the close of an early scene, the 'traveller in spells,' crouching down, made an extraordinary exit, in imitation of a railway train, holding a 'fizzing' teapot. A tumultuous roar of applause greeted the ingenious artist.[1]

---

[1] It is said that this was as much a surprise for his brethren as it was for the audience, and that this effective piece of business was kept dark until the night in question.

The public is often as indiscriminate in its partialities as it is in its dislikes, and during the course of these early operas was thrown into convulsions of delight by a rather simple device of the composer's. This was the introduction of a grotesque passage, a 'remark,' as it were, of the bassoon's, uttered during some 'patter song.' The bassoon has been called 'the clown of the orchestra'—a happy description in the case of comic opera.

The 'Sorcerer,' among its other welcome enjoyments, contributed some effective and quotable things which constantly do duty in the newspapers. Such was the chorus at the end :

> Now to the banquet we press—
> 　Now for the eggs and the ham—
> Now for the mustard and cress—
> 　Now for the strawberry jam !

CHORUS. Now to the banquet, &c.

Dr. Daly, Constance, Notary, *and* Mrs. Partlet

Now for the tea of our host—
Now for *the rollicking bun*—
Now for the muffin and toast—
Now for *the gay Sally Lunn*!

Chorus. Now for the tea, &c.

This humour is specially 'Gilbertian.' There is something grotesque in this exuberant praise of the

Sally Lunn and bun which would bring a rueful smile to the face even of the most dyspeptic. The 'rollicking bun' has become 'a common form.'

The success of this experiment—and it was little more than an experiment—encouraged the partners to give yet fuller play to their special talent, and they were now busy with a more elaborate effort—the admirable 'Pinafore.'

First produced on the night of May 28, 1878

H.M.S. PINAFORE

Dramatis Personæ

The Rt. Hon. Sir Joseph Porter, K.C.B. *(First Lord of the Admiralty)* . .	Mr. George Grossmith
Capt. Corcoran *(commanding H.M.S. Pinafore)*	Mr. Rutland Barrington
Ralph Rackstraw *(Able Seaman)* . .	Mr. George Power
Dick Deadeye *(Able Seaman)* . . .	Mr. Richard Temple
Bill Bobstay *(Boatswain's Mate)* . .	Mr. Clifton
Josephine *(the Captain's Daughter)* .	Miss Emma Howson
Hebe	Miss Jessie Bond
Little Buttercup *(a Portsmouth Bumboat Woman)*	Miss Everard

First Lord's Sisters, his Cousins, his Aunts, Sailors, Marines, &c.

SCENE.—Quarterdeck of **H.M.S.** Pinafore, off Portsmouth

ACT I.—Noon.   ACT II.—Night

There is a long list of young ladies who essayed the part of Josephine—to wit, Miss Emma Howson, Miss A. Burville, Miss Blanche Roosevelt, Miss Mulholland, Miss Pauline Rita, and Miss Kate Sullivan.

This opera was, perhaps, the most genuinely successful of the whole series, for it was more seen, talked of, chanted, hummed, and quoted than all of its fellows, except, perhaps, the 'Mikado.' Everyone was delighted with it. Its good things were irresistibly, though quietly, droll. At the outset it rather hung fire. I

must confess with some shame that at my first visit
it appeared to me a little forced and far-fetched. But
presently it became 'all the rage,' and the actors,
catching the enthusiasm, threw themselves with ardour
into their work. *C'était immense!* and the opera ran
for nearly a couple of years, to say nothing of its
regular promenade round the country.

The story is of the slightest, but more than sufficient. In these things Gilbert's touch is of the most
airy kind ; he indicates rather than describes. He sets
out a sketch of sea life with sea characters, such as the
inimitable First Lord, the captain, the bos'un's mate,
the 'bumboat woman,'[1] and the gruesome Dick Deadeye.
The First Lord has a dim notion of wedding the
captain's fair daughter, who is attached to Ralph
Rackstraw, that 'common' sailor, the epithet seeming
to her a bit of fine irony. The author is fond of
dwelling on a favourite utopian theory—a reversal of the
different classes of society, showing the oddities that
result from a change of position. The bumboat woman
reveals that she had changed the 'common sailor' with
the captain at nurse, who accordingly at the close take
up their proper positions. But as I said, the story is
nothing. It is the characters and humour that attract.

[1] Whenever I went on board, he would beckon me down below.
    'Come down, Little Buttercup, come ' (for he loved to call me so).
                                    The Bumboat Woman's Story.

Here, too, like the author of ' Pickwick,' Gilbert has furnished sayings which have become the currency of social life. Nothing gave the public more enjoyment —and the saying is still in favour—than the ' What, never ?   Well, hardly ever ! ' of the captain.

> Though related to a peer,
> I can haul, reef, and steer,
>   And ship a selvagee ;
> I am never known to quail
> At the fury of a gale,
>   And I'm never, never sick at sea !
>   ALL. What, never ?
>   CAPT. No, *never*!
>   ALL. What, never ?
>   CAPT. Hardly ever !
>   ALL. He's hardly ever sick at sea !
>   Then give three cheers, &c.

And again :

> Bad language or abuse
> I never, never use,
>   Whatever the emergency ;
> Though ' Bother it ! ' I may
> Occasionally say,
>   I never use a big, big D.[1]

This ' big, big D ' also became a stock phrase.   The expressive music to the interrogation, ' What, never ? ' will be recalled.

[1] When Jack Tars growl, I believe they growl
        With a big, big D ——
    But the strongest oath of the Hot Cross Bun
        Was a mild, ' Dear me ! '— *Bab Ballads*.

The ' Ruler of the Queen's Navee ' is known to every-one, and has done service in newspapers, in talk, and in Parliament. Seldom, indeed, has there been a happier combination than in this character. There were capital good things to say, capital music to sing, and a capital comedian to sustain the part. The spare, wiry figure of Grossmith, with his whitened hair and blue uniform, his dignified bearing, quiet and distinct voicing, was long enjoyed by the public. The satire, exaggerated as it was, told; the official methods were good-naturedly ridiculed. This tranquil reserve is with our author always preparatory to a mirth-moving con-trast.

The First Lord thus introduces himself :

> I am the monarch of the sea,
> The ruler of the Queen's Navee,
> Whose praise Great Britain loudly chants.

COUSIN HEBE

And we are his sisters, and his cousins, and his aunts !

REL.

And we are his sisters, and his cousins, and his aunts !

SIR JOSEPH

> But when the breezes blow,
> I generally go below,
> *And seek the seclusion that a cabin grants !*

COUSIN HEBE

And so do his sisters, and his cousins, and his aunts !

F

ALL

And so do his sisters, and his cousins, and his aunts.
His sisters and his cousins,
Whom he reckons up by dozens,
And his aunts!

The briny spirit of this capital song was caught to
perfection by the composer. The opening, with its stately
Handelian treatment, contrasted with the pleasantly
exuberant intrusion of the female voices, ' And we are
his sisters, and his cousins, and his aunts,' so pert and
rollicking. This, again, has become a popular quotation.[1]
How lively, too, is Sir Joseph's lesson of politeness with
which he goes off:

For I hold that on the seas,
The expression, ' if you please,'
A particularly gentlemanly tone imparts.

[1] Then up and answered William Lee
(The kindly captain's coxswain he,
A nervous, shy, low-spoken man),
He cleared his throat and thus began :

' You have a daughter, Captain Reece,
Ten female cousins and a niece,
A ma, if what I'm told is true,
Six sisters, and an aunt or two.

' If you'd ameliorate our life,
Let each select from them a wife ;
And as for nervous me, old pal,
Give me your own enchanting gal !'

Good Captain Reece, that worthy man,
Debated on his coxswain's plan :
' I quite agree,' he said, ' O Bill ;
It is my duty, and I will.'

' Captain Reece,' in *Bab Ballads*.

There was an animation and humour in these trifling words, and the strains even now ring pleasantly in our ears.

Another often-quoted saying is the boast of being an Englishman:

> He is an Englishman!
> For he himself has said it,
> And it's greatly to his credit
> That he is an Englishman!
> That he is an Englishman!
> For he might have been a Roosian,
> A French, or Turk, or Proosian,
> Or perhaps Itali-an!
> Or perhaps Itali-an!
> But in spite of all temptations
> To belong to other nations,
> He remains an Englishman!

The grotesqueness of this declaration is excellent satire on *frondeur* vauntings. Almost as good is the fine contrapuntal strain of the music, with its stately close.

One of the regular forms of the Gilbertian opera is the fantastic dance into which the gravest, most decorous characters burst tumultuously. These measures have yet a quaint reserve, as though extorted from the personages in question by the irresistible *entrain* of the situation. Such was the trio between the captain, the First Lord, and Josephine:

CAPTAIN

Never mind the why and wherefore,
Love can level ranks, and therefore,
Though his lordship's station's mighty,
    Though stupendous be his brain,
Though your tastes are mean and flighty,
    And your fortune poor and plain,

CAPTAIN AND SIR JOSEPH

Ring the merry bells on board-ship,
Rend the air with warbling wild,
For the union of $\left\{ \begin{array}{l} his \\ my \end{array} \right\}$ lordship
With a humble captain's child !

CAPT. For a humble captain's daughter—
Jos. (*aside*). For a gallant captain's daughter.
SIR JOSEPH. And a lord who rules the water—
Jos. (*aside*). And a *tar* who ploughs the water.

ALL

Let the air with joy be laden,
    Rend with songs the air above,
For the union of a maiden
    With a man who owns her love.

The music here was delightful, particularly where the characters answer each other in deprecating fashion :

For a humble captain's daughter—
And a lord who rules the water—
And a tar who ploughs the water.

Which led to the melodious chime—

Ring the merry bells, &c.

which in its turn brought on the fantastic and most original dance. How many times that used to be called for and repeated!

But the words without their expressive music lose half their effect. As we read them the strains flutter on the ear. Thus with Buttercup's song:

DUET—LITTLE BUTTERCUP AND CAPTAIN

BUTTERCUP

Things are seldom what they seem,
Skim milk masquerades as cream;
Highlows pass as patent leathers;
Jackdaws strut in peacocks' feathers.

CAPT. (*puzzled*). Very true,
   So they do.

BUTTERCUP

Black sheep dwell in every fold;
All that glitters is not gold;
Storks turn out to be but logs;
Bulls are but inflated frogs.

CAPT. (*puzzled*). So they be,
   Frequentlee.

Here the notes of ' Very true,' &c., are most appropriate. Gilbert's rhymes, too, how free and easy!

   Sailors sprightly,
   Always rightly
   Welcome ladies so politely.

and again—

   Gaily tripping,
   Lightly skipping,

Flock the maidens to the shipping,
Flags and guns and pennants dipping—
All the ladies love the shipping.

It is only when we think of the more conventional libretto that we see the novelty of the thing; the words asserting themselves equally with the music and requiring to be taken seriously.

Gilbert, too, excels in imparting a gravity to some platitude. As when Buttercup hesitatingly reveals her love, the captain replies tranquilly, 'Ah, Little Buttercup, still on board; that is not quite right, little one. It would have been more respectable to have gone on shore before dusk'; and when Josephine reveals to her father her love for the 'common sailor,' he soothes her: 'Come, my child, let us talk this over. In a matter of the heart I would not coerce my daughter. I attach but little value to rank or wealth—*but the line must be drawn somewhere.*'

There have since been revivals of these old favourites, such as the 'Sorcerer,' 'H.M.S. Pinafore,' the 'Mikado,' 'Trial by Jury,' and on each occasion great efforts were made to excel in mounting and decoration all previous displays.[1] It would seem, however, to be the result of the 'form and pressure of the time' that

---

In the 'Pinafore' a regular deck-flooring was laid down, and a perfect reproduction of a man-of-war constructed, under the direction of qualified persons from the dockyards.

revivals rarely answer save under special conditions. Where the work has been thoroughly appreciated, the very familiarity and the enjoyment of its good things work against it : the recollection is too fresh—even after the interval of almost a generation there is a suggestion of old fashion. In light comic opera music, too, its forms reflect the impression of the moment, and have become familiar from constant imitation and repetition, until at last the attraction is altogether exhausted. This is particularly felt where phrases have become part and parcel of the language, such as the ' hardly ever ' allusions reproduced in ' Utopia.' We are apt to exclaim ' *Connu !* ' We have had some recent revivals of comic operas, such as ' Madame Angot,' ' Madame Favart,' and the like, and it was difficult to listen to them without this sense of ' flatness ' and staleness.[1]

---

[1] At a late revival the cast was :

H.M.S. PINAFORE
OR
THE LASS THAT LOVED A SAILOR

Dramatis Personæ

THE RT. HON. SIR JOSEPH PORTER, K.C.B.
    (*First Lord of the Admiralty*) . . MR. GEORGE GROSSMITH
CAPT. CORCORAN (*commanding H.M.S.*
    Pinafore) . . . . . . MR. RUTLAND BARRINGTON
RALPH RACKSTRAW (*Able Seaman*) . . MR. J. G. ROBERTSON
DICK DEADEYE (*Able Seaman*) . . . MR. RICHARD TEMPLE
BILL BOBSTAY (*Boatswain's Mate*) . . MR. R. CUMMINGS

It is amusing at this distance of time to read the sort
of reserved criticism and measured encouragement with
which these works were received, and which contrast with
the present hearty approbation which welcomes every
effort of the authors. A truly absurd appreciation was that
of a well-known journal, which gravely announced that the
last portion of the title might have been omitted with advantage, and that it should have stood simply 'H.M.S.'

Most of these operas are peculiarly acceptable to
amateurs; and it can scarcely be conceived to what an
extent they have been performed under these conditions.
Every leading *comique* of the private stage feels himself
drawn to reproduce Grossmith as the First Lord in
'Pinafore.' The management and proprietors of the
copyright, though jealous enough in enforcing their
strict rights, have always shown themselves liberal in
these cases, especially where a charity is in question.
One of the most successful of these productions was a
performance given at Dublin Castle some years ago,

Bob BECKET (*Carpenter's Mate*) . . .	Mr. R. LEWIS
JOSEPHINE (*the Captain's Daughter*) . .	MISS GERALDINE ULMAR
HEBE (*Sir Joseph's First Cousin*) . . .	MISS JESSIE BOND
LITTLE BUTTERCUP (*a Portsmouth Bumboat Woman*)	MISS ROSINA BRANDRAM

FIRST LORD'S SISTERS, HIS COUSINS, HIS AUNTS, SAILORS,
MARINES, &c.

SCENE.—Quarterdeck of H.M.S. Pinafore,
off Portsmouth

ACT I.—Noon.   ACT. II.—Night.

in honour of the Duke of Edinburgh, who was on a visit there, and in aid of the prevailing Irish distress. It was excellently played, Sir Joseph Porter being admirably given by Captain McCalmont, M.P., and the heroine by Miss Geraldine FitzGerald. It was really a brilliant spectacle, and was repeated several times with excellent pecuniary results.[1]

After two years' interval, during which time the public had thoroughly learned to appreciate its entertainers and their methods, a fresh opera was presented.

Produced at the Opera Comique Theatre, London, Saturday, April 3, 1880, under the management of Mr. R. D'Oyly Carte

THE PIRATES OF PENZANCE

Dramatis Personæ

MAJOR-GENERAL STANLEY	MR. GEORGE GROSSMITH
THE PIRATE KING	MR. RICHARD TEMPLE
SAMUEL (*his Lieutenant*) . . .	MR. GEORGE TEMPLE
FREDERIC (*the Pirate Apprentice*) . .	MR. GEORGE POWER
SERGEANT OF POLICE	MR. RUTLAND BARRINGTON
MABEL	MISS MARION HOOD
EDITH (*General Stanley's Daughters*)	MISS BOND
KATE	MISS GWYNNE
ISABEL	MISS LA RUE
RUTH (*a Private Maid-of-all-Work*) . .	MISS EMILY CROSS

Chorus of Pirates, Police, and General Stanley's Daughters.

The 'Pirates of Penzance' seems one of the most piquant and picturesque events of the series. There is

---

[1] At schools, too, these pieces are in great demand. Some time ago, at one of our great colleges, where nearly the whole series has been performed, a professor rewrote and refitted one of the operas, introducing

a colour about it, with a genuine and piquant story.
Like the 'Sorcerer,' it was suggested by an allusion
in one of the old 'Bab Ballads,' and was based on a
characteristic Gilbertian idea—viz. that of a band of
pirates whose proceedings were regulated by a sort of
topsy-turvy *logic*.   Thus they sing :

> Pour, O pour the pirate sherry ;
>   Fill, O fill the pirate glass :
> And to make us more the merry,
>   Let the pirate bumper pass.
> For to-day our pirate 'prentice
>   Rises, from indenture freed :
> Strong his arm and keen his scent is,
>   He's a pirate now indeed !
> ALL. Here's good luck to Frederic's ventures,
>   Frederic's out of his indentures.

Frederic, a rather pedantic young pirate, and which
was performed by George Power in an interesting fashion
and with due sincerity, is described : ' a keener hand at
scuttling a Cunarder, or cutting out a White Star, never
shipped a handspike.'   Ruth is attached to him, whom
he describes as ' the remains of a fine woman.'   A bevy
of young girls find their way to the pirates' den, who

lyrics of his own, and shaping the whole on entirely new lines. He
was so confiding as to forward a copy to the author, reckoning on
sympathy and commendation even. It need not be said he little
knew Mr. Gilbert, and still less recked of the sound ' wigging ' he
was to receive for this tampering. The poor professor was scared by
hearing of impending pains and penalties.

THE PIRATES OF PENZANCE

prove to be the daughters of ' Major-General Stanley '
—who is a happy specimen of our author's method
of dealing with such characters. There is something
quaintly ' impossible ' about him, and yet he is plausible.
An ordinary writer dealing with him must have followed
the conventional lines of grotesque military command :
and we all know the typical *bouffe* military general, who
in an exaggerated costume will utter grotesque sayings
and exhibit pantomime dances and songs. But this
major-general is intellectually grotesque.

The pirates surround them, when this droll and
really dramatic situation follows :

> PIRATES
> Here's a first-rate opportunity
> To get married with impunity,
> And indulge in the felicity
> Of unbounded domesticity.
> You shall quickly be parsonified,
> Conjugally matrimonified,
> By a doctor of divinity
> Who resides in this vicinity.

Then Mabel, one of his daughters, gives this caution :

> Hold, monsters ! Ere your pirate caravanserai
> Proceed, against our will, to wed us all,
> Just bear in mind that we are wards in Chancery,
> And father is a major-general !
>> SAMUEL (*cowed*)
> We'd better pause, or danger may befall ;
> Their father is a major-general.

LADIES. Yes, yes; he is a major-general! (*The* MAJOR-
GENERAL *has entered unnoticed on rock.*)

GEN. Yes, I am a major-general!

ALL. You are!
> Hurrah for the major-general!

GEN. And it is—it is a glorious thing
> To be a major-general!

ALL. It is!
> Hurrah for the major-general!

The major-general tells his story according to the
approved form :

> I am the very pattern of a modern major-general,
> I've information vegetable, animal, and mineral ;
> I know the kings of England, and I quote the fights
> > historical,
> From Marathon to Waterloo, in order categorical ;
> I'm very well acquainted, too, with matters mathematical,
> I understand equations, both the simple and quadratical,
> About binomial theorem I'm teeming with a lot o' news—
> With many cheerful facts about the square of the hypote-
> > nuse.

ALL. With many cheerful facts, &c.

GENERAL

> I'm very good at integral and differential calculus,
> I know the scientific names of beings animalculous,
> In short, in matters vegetable, animal, and mineral,
> I am the very model of a modern major-general.

ALL

> In short, in matters vegetable, animal, and mineral,
> He is the very model of a modern major-general.

And so on. This was an extraordinary specimen of the
'patter' song, continued for many verses and delivered

with equal rapidity and accuracy by Grossmith. A principle of the pirates in their business is to be merciful to all 'orphans,' they being orphans themselves; and it was reasonably urged that this bit of humanitarianism seriously interfered with profits, as everyone pleaded orphanage, the major-general among the rest.

GEN. (*aside*). And do you mean to say that you would deliberately rob me of these the sole remaining props of my old age, and leave me to go through the remainder of my life unfriended, unprotected, and alone?

KING. *Well, yes, that's the idea.*

GEN. I ask you, have you ever known what it is to be an orphan?

KING. Often!

GEN. Yes, orphan. Have you ever known what it is to be one?

KING. I say, often.

ALL (*disgusted*). Often, often, often (*turning away*).

GEN. I don't think we quite understand one another. I ask you, have you ever known what it is to be an orphan, and you say 'orphan.' As I understand you, you are merely repeating the word 'orphan' to show that you understand me.

KING. I didn't repeat the word often.

GEN. Pardon me, you did indeed.

KING. I only repeated it once.

GEN. True, but you repeated it.

KING. But not often.

GEN. Stop, I think I see where we are getting confused. When you said 'orphan,' did you mean 'orphan,' a person who has lost his parents, or often—frequently?

KING. Ah, I beg pardon, I see what you mean—frequently.

GEN. Ah, you said often—frequently.

KING. No, only once.

GEN. (*irritated*). Exactly, you said often, frequently, only once.

This is perhaps too fragile for the stage, but still is amusing. A body of pirates naturally suggests other bodies who control them. Here was the author's opportunity for introducing the police, a topic handled with much humour. There is really nothing better than all the passages dealing with the 'Force,' and the naïve expression of their emotions—not at all far-fetched—is delightful.

(*Enter* POLICE, *marching in double file. They form in line facing audience*)

SERGEANT

When the foeman bares his steel,
    Tarantara, tarantara!
We uncomfortable feel,
    Tarantara!
And we find the wisest thing,
    Tarantara, tarantara!
Is to slap our chests and sing
    Tarantara!
For when threatened with *émeutes*,
    Tarantara, tarantara!
And your heart is in your boots,
    Tarantara!
There is nothing brings it round,
    Tarantara, tarantara!
Like the trumpet's martial sound,
    Tarantara, tarantara!
Tarantara, ra-ra-ra-ra!

ALL. Tarantara, ra-ra-ra ra!

Mabel

Go, ye heroes, go to glory,
Though you die in combat gory
Ye shall live in song and story.
Go to immortality.
Go to death, and go to slaughter;
Die, and every Cornish daughter
With her tears your grave shall water.
Go, ye heroes; go and die.

ALL. Go, ye heroes; go and die.

Police

Though to us it's evident,
Tarantara, tarantara!
These attentions are well meant,
Tarantara!
Such expressions don't appear,
Tarantara, tarantara
Calculated men to cheer,
Tarantara!
Who are going to meet their fate
In a highly nervous state,
Tarantara!
Still to us it's evident
These attentions are well meant.
Tarantara!

(Edith *crosses to* Serg. C.)

Edith

Go, and do your best endeavour,
And before all links we sever,
We will say farewell for ever,
Go to glory and the grave!

ALL. Yes, your foes are fierce and ruthless.

Sergeant

We observe too great a stress
On the risks that on us press,
And of reference a lack
To our chance of coming back ;
Still, perhaps it would be wise
Not to carp or criticise,
For it's very evident
These attentions are well meant.

All

Yes, to them it's evident
Our attentions are well meant.
        Tarantara, ra-ra-ra-ra.
Go, ye heroes, go to glory, &c.

GEN. Away, away !
POLICE (*without moving*). Yes, yes, we go.
GEN. These pirates slay.
POLICE.   Yes, yes, we go.
GEN. Then do not stay.
POLICE.   We go, we go.
GEN. Then why all this delay ?

Police

    All right—we go, we go.
  Yes, forward on the foe,
      Ho, ho ! Ho, ho !
  We go, we go, we go !
      Tarantara-ra-ra !
  Then forward on the foe !
ALL. Yes, forward !
POLICE. Yes, forward !
GEN. Yes, but you *don't* go !
POLICE. We go, we go, we go !
ALL. At last they really go—Tarantara-ra-ra.

This rises almost to the style of grand opera, and
the contrast between the stirring strains of encouragement 'Go! Go!' and the mild protest of 'the Force'
is in the best style of burlesque.   The music, too, is
finely wrought and 'worked up' into a telling *stretto*.
Later, the Force is constantly 'heard approaching,' and
their solemn 'tramping' strains are most effective and
stirring.

(*Enter* POLICE, *marching in single file*)

SERGEANT

Though in body and in mind,
   Tarantara, tarantara!
We are timidly inclined,
   Tarantara!
And anything but blind,
   Tarantara, tarantara!
To the danger that's behind,
   Tarantara!
Yet, when the danger's near,
   Tarantara, tarantara!
We manage to appear,
   Tarantara!
As insensible to fear
As anybody here.
   Tarantara, tarantara, ra-ra-ra-ra!

Who will forget, too, the sergeant's song:

When a felon's not engaged in his employment,
ALL.   His employment.
SERG. Or maturing his felonious little plans,
ALL.   Little plans.

SERGEANT

His capacity for innocent enjoyment
Is just as great as any honest man's.
Our feelings we with difficulty smother
When constabulary duty's to be done ;
Ah, take one consideration with another,
A policeman's lot is not a happy one.

When the enterprising burglar's not a-burgling,
When the cutthroat isn't occupied in crime,
He loves to hear the little brook a-gurgling,
And listen to the merry village chime.
When the coster's finished jumping on his mother,
He loves to lie a-basking in the sun ;
Ah, take one consideration with another,
The policeman's lot is not a happy one.[1]

This capital song has become a general favourite.
The taking 'one consideration with another, the policeman's lot is not a happy one,' the coster 'jumping on
his mother,' and the 'burgling' are perpetual topics for
quotation.[2]

At the time the next opera was being prepared—viz.
in 1881—the community was afflicted by what was
called the æsthetic craze, which, as is well known, was
inspired by that clever personage Mr. Oscar Wilde, a

[1] A grotesque element in this droll song was the repetition by
the constables of the last words—syllables, rather—of each line, often
with very original emphasis and effect, such as, ' 'culty smother,' 'a-
gurgling,' and ' 'cent enjoyment.'

[2] I have been assured, too, that these passages are in equal favour
with the Force itself, and their lot not being ' a happy one ' is frequently
quoted.

man who has since proved himself the possessor of some really solid gifts. There was a jargon then used by followers of the cult of which the phrase 'quite too utter' was a fair specimen. All this has now passed away. Naturally it tempted the satirists, Burnand and Du Maurier, whose Postlethwaite and Maudle and the 'Cimabue Browns' had already been diverting the town. 'Patience' was exceedingly popular, and the absurd figure of Bunthorne with his sunflower and attendant troupe of admiring 'damosels' was highly humorous. It certainly helped to 'kill off' the mania.

Produced at the Opera Comique, London, on Saturday,
April 23, 1881, under the management of Mr. R. D'Oyly Carte

PATIENCE

or

BUNTHORNE'S BRIDE

Dramatis Personæ

Reginald Bunthorne (*a Fleshly Poet*)	.	Mr. George Grossmith
Archibald Grosvenor (*an Idyllic Poet*)	.	Mr. Rutland Barrington
Colonel Calverley		Mr. Walter Browne
Major Murgatroyd	(*Officers of Dragoon Guards*)	Mr. Frank Thornton
Lieut. the Duke of Dunstable		Mr. Durward Lely

Chorus of Officers of Dragoon Guards.

The Lady Angela		Miss Jessie Bond
The Lady Saphir	(*Rapturous Maidens*)	Miss Julia Gwynne
The Lady Ella		Miss Fortescue
The Lady Jane		Miss Alice Barnett
Patience (*a Dairy Maid*)		Miss Leonora Braham

Chorus of Rapturous Maidens.

ACT I.—Exterior of Castle Bunthorne

ACT II.—A Glade

Musical Conductor	. . . . . .	Mr. FRANK CELLIER
Stage Manager	. . . . . .	Mr. W. H. SEYMOUR

The opera produced under the personal direction of the author and composer. New scenery by H. EMDEN. The æsthetic dresses designed by the author and executed by MISS FISHER. Other dresses by MESSRS. MOSES & SON, MESSRS. G. HOBSON & Co., and MADAME AUGUSTE. The dances arranged by MR. J. D'AUBAN.

At 8 a new and original Vaudeville, by FRANK DESPREZ, music by EATON FANNING, called

MOCK TURTLES

MR. WRANGLEBURY	. . . . .	MR. ARTHUR LAW
MRS. WRANGLEBURY	. . . .	MISS MINNA LOUIS
MRS. BOWCHER	. . . . .	MISS BRANDRAM
JANE	. . . . . .	MISS SYBIL GREY

No fees of any kind.

Acting Manager	. . . . .	MR. GEORGE EDWARDES

The music in 'Patience' attracted a large class of admirers, I believe, on account of its many taking ballads and tunes. Numbers—even the more unmusical —were attracted by such songs as the 'Silver Churn,' which they sang or tried to sing. Even officers and prosaic beings of all kinds contrived to 'hum' or growl this taking melody. I have often thought that here was a hint of which note might have been profitably taken, and that this element of popularity might have been more steadily developed. But the fact is that in later productions the composer seemed to depart further and yet further from the original model. He appeared

to strive more after broad musical effects, developed
choruses and finales, after the pattern of grand
opera. If we look through all these works we shall
find that tunes of the ballad pattern have been what
attracted the public most.

SHALL HAVE TO BE CONTENTED   WITH THEIR HEARTFELT SYMPATHY!"

We have seen that Gilbert's method of devising
choruses is original enough, because he individualises
them. There is something very piquant in the group of
officers belonging to the 35th Dragoons. We always
welcome the honest fellows as they enter. They have

double the effect of a large professional chorus. How
pleasantly, and legitimately, too, the author plays with
the slight topic of uniform ! One would think that little
could be made of such a theme :

DUKE. We didn't design our uniforms, but we don't see
how they could be improved.

SONG—COLONEL

When I first put this uniform on,
I said, as I looked in the glass,
' It's one to a million
That any civilian
My figure and form will surpass.
Gold lace has a charm for the fair,
And I've plenty of that, and to spare,
While a lover's professions,
When uttered in hessians,
Are eloquent everywhere !'
A fact that I counted upon
When I first put this uniform on !

CHORUS OF DRAGOONS

By a simple coincidence few
Could ever have reckoned upon,
The same thing occurred to me, too,
When I first put this uniform on !

COLONEL

I said, when I first put it on,
' It is plain to the veriest dunce
That every beauty
Will feel it her duty
To yield to its glamour at once.

They will see that I'm freely gold-laced
In a uniform handsome and chaste '—
   But the peripatetics
   Of long-haired æsthetics
Are very much more to their taste—
    Which I never counted upon
    When I first put this uniform on !

CHORUS
By a simple coincidence few
   Could ever have counted upon,
I didn't anticipate that,
   When I first put this uniform on.

The dignity of the notion ' *When I first put this uni-form on* ' is pleasantly expressed by the spirited, martial clang of the tune, which almost exactly conveys the sentiment. In the description of the æsthetical youth the authors revel :

TWO LOVE-SICK MAIDENS

A most intense young man,
A soulful-eyed young man,
An ultra-poetical, super-æsthetical,
Out-of-the-way young man.

A Japanese young man,
A blue and white young man,
Francesca di Rimini, niminy, piminy,
Je-ne-sais-quoi young man.

A Chancery Lane young man,
A Somerset House young man,

"I'M A STEADY AND STOLID-Y,
Jolly BANK-HOLIDY
EVERY-DAY YOUNG MAN!"

A very delectable, highly respectable,
Threepenny-bus young man.

A pallid and thin young man,
A haggard and lank young man,
*A greenery-yallery, Grosvenor Gallery,
Foot-in-the-grave young man.*

MISS L. BRAHAM AS PATIENCE

A Sewell and Cross young man,
A Howell and James young man,
A pushing young particle—what's the next article?
Waterloo House young man.

ENSEMBLE

BUNTHORNE

Conceive me, if you can,
A crotchety, cracked young man,
An ultra-poetical, super-æsthetical,
Out-of-the-way young man.

GROSVENOR

Conceive me, if you can,
A matter-of-fact young man,
An alphabetical, arithmetical,
Every-day young man.

The exuberant fertility with which the idea is here varied will be noted. The 'greenery-yallery, Grosvenor Gallery,' for rhyme and point is first rate, and has justly become proverbial.

At the close of the piece the hero becomes

An every-day young man,
A commonplace type
With a stick and a pipe,
And a half-bred black and tan.

A suggestion of the story is found in that lively 'Bab Ballad' the 'Rival Curates,' wherein the Rev. Hopley Parker figures.[1]

Some of the humorous topics were insisted on, to the sacrifice of the sense of refinement. The verses on 'Colocynth and Calomel' we

ÆSTHETIC! HE IS ÆSTHETIC!
YES, YES — I AM ÆSTHETIC
AND POETIC!

This tide of prosperity suggested a larger and more ambitious scheme and an important change of methods. The contracted Opera Comique, with its stinted accommodation, was quite unsuited to the run of popularity which the associates might count upon. The shrewd and adventurous D'Oyly Carte was now planning a theatre that was to be specially suited to this new *genre* of opera. Everything was carefully mapped out and calculated—the situation, size and arrangement—and the plans of a beautiful and costly building were being

could have wished away. An over-delicate critic, indeed, was shocked at the word 'fleshly.' A tall and somewhat portly lady, with a good voice, who made a semblance of accompanying herself on the violoncello, was made to dwell rather too persistently on her physical gifts. Such topics do not appeal to the humorous sense, and are something of a humiliation for the performer. Her appeal to her admirer—rather, to the person she admired—is, however, exceedingly humorous: 'But do not dally too long, Reginald; for I am ripe, Reginald, and already I am decaying. *Better secure me ere I have gone too far.*' It must be flattering to the author to find that the freaks of what has been called his 'topsyturveydom,' though presumed to be confined to the land of dreams and nightmares, are constantly reproduced in the matter-of-fact course of life. Thus the consequences of a union of offices in one person was grotesquely illustrated in the *Mikado*; and, in the discussion on the Parish Councils Bill, it was pointed out that ' one body acting as a parish council will have to report to itself, acting as a district council, that allotments are wanted. It will then, acting as a district council, inquire into the accuracy of its own report as a parish council. A situation,' added the speaker, ' worthy of Gilbert and Sullivan.' And not long since, a well-known Liverpool magistrate was summoned with others for an offence. 'Can I fine myself?' he asked. It was suggested that he should inflict double the usual penalty. The new Pooh-Bah accordingly fined himself, and then administered a severe rebuke to himself and to the other culprits !

matured. It was difficult, however, to procure a site, and a suitable one was at last found between the Strand and the Embankment, and in the precincts of the old Savoy. The patch of ground was not very large, and rather awkwardly situated on a steep descent with inconvenient approaches, wedged in, as it were, among surrounding buildings. It had to be reached through a sort of tunnel. Yet with all these inconveniences the ingenuity of the architect and owner contrived that it should have approaches on three sides at least. The chief portion of the interior, like that of the Criterion, was excavated; and the stage lay far below the street level. Though many new theatres have since been erected—and Gilbert himself has indulged in the luxury of building one—none have surpassed the Savoy in elegance, comfort, or even luxuriousness.[1]

---

[1] On the eve of the opening our manager issued an address to the public, setting forth his views, adding also a minute account of the details of construction. It will be noted that he claims that this was the first theatre which was lighted throughout, both stage and auditorium, by electricity.

To the Public

LADIES AND GENTLEMEN,—I beg leave to lay before you some details of a new theatre, which I have caused to be built with the intention of devoting it to the representation of the operas of Messrs. W. S. Gilbert and Arthur Sullivan, with whose joint productions I have, up to now, had the advantage of being associated.

The Savoy Theatre is placed between the Strand and the Victoria Embankment, on a plot of land of which I have purchased the freehold, and is built on a spot possessing many associations of historic interest,

I recall the night after the theatre was finished and ready to open, when a number of friends and

being close to the Savoy Chapel and in the 'precinct of the Savoy,' where stood formerly the Savoy Palace, once inhabited by John of Gaunt and the Dukes of Lancaster, and made memorable in the Wars of the Roses. On the Savoy Manor there was formerly a theatre. I have used the ancient name as an appropriate title for the present one.

The new theatre has been erected from the designs and under the superintendence of Mr. C. J. Phipps, F.S.A., who has probably more experience in the building of such places than any architect of past or present times, having put up, I believe, altogether thirty-three or thirty-four theatres.

The façade of the theatre towards the Embankment, and that in Beaufort Buildings, are of red brick and Portland stone. The theatre is large and commodious, but little smaller than the Gaiety, and will seat 1,292 persons.

I think I may claim to have carried out some improvements deserving special notice. The most important of these are in the lighting and decoration.

From the time, now some years since, that the first electric lights in lamps were exhibited outside the Paris Opera House, I have been convinced that electric light in some form is the light of the future for use in theatres, not to go further. The peculiar steely blue colour and the flicker which are inevitable in all systems of 'arc' lights, however, make them unsuitable for use in any but very large buildings. The invention of the 'incandescent lamp' has now paved the way for the application of electricity to lighting houses, and consequently theatres.

The 'arc' light is simply a continuous electric spark, and is nearly the colour of lightning. The incandescent light is produced by heating a filament of carbon to a white heat, and is much the colour of gas—a little clearer. Thanks to an ingenious method of 'shunting' it, the current is easily controllable, and the lights can be raised or lowered at will. There are several extremely good incandescent lamps, but I finally decided to adopt that of Mr. J. W. Swan, the well-known inventor, of Newcastle-on-Tyne. The enterprise of Messrs. Siemens Bros. & Co. has enabled me to try the experiment of exhibiting this light in my theatre. About 1,200 lights are used, and the power to generate a sufficient current for these is obtained from large steam-engines, giving

critics, with others distinctly or indistinctly connected
with the stage, attended to observe and admire, and

about 120 horse-power, placed on some open land near the theatre. The
new light is not only used in the audience part of the theatre, but on
the stage, for footlights, side and top lights, &c., and (not of the least
importance for the comfort of the performers) in the dressing-rooms—in
fact, in every part of the house. This is the first time that it has been
attempted to light any public building entirely by electricity. What is
being done is an experiment, and may succeed, or fail. It is not possible,
until the application of the accumulator or secondary battery—the reserve store of electric power—becomes practicable, to guarantee absolutely against any breakdown of the electric light. To provide against
such a contingency gas is laid on throughout the building, and the
' pilot ' light of the central sun-burner will be always kept alight, so that
in case of accident the theatre can be flooded with gaslight in a few
seconds. The greatest drawbacks to the enjoyment of theatrical performances are, undoubtedly, the foul air and heat which pervade all
theatres. As everyone knows, each gas-burner consumes as much oxygen
as many people, and causes great heat besides. The incandescent lamps
consume *no* oxygen, and cause no perceptible heat. If the experiment
of electric lighting succeeds, there can be no question of the enormous
advantages to be gained in purity of air and coolness—advantages the
value of which it is hardly possible to over-estimate.

The decorations of this theatre are by Messrs. Collinson & Lock.

I venture to think that, with some few exceptions, the interiors of
most theatres hitherto built have been conceived with little, if any,
artistic purpose, and generally executed with little completeness, and
in a more or less garish manner. Without adopting either of the styles
known as ' Queen Anne ' and ' Early English,' or entering upon the so-
called ' æsthetic ' manner, a result has now been produced which I feel
sure will be appreciated by all persons of taste. Paintings of cherubim,
muses, angels, and mythological deities have been discarded, and the
ornament consists entirely of delicate plaster modelling, designed in the
manner of the Italian Renaissance. The main colour-tones are white,
pale yellow, and gold—gold used only for backgrounds or in large
masses, and not—following what may be called, for want of a worse
name, the Gingerbread school of decorative art—for gilding relief-work
or mouldings. The back walls of the boxes and the corridors are in two

loud was the admiration expressed. On October 10, 1881, the theatre opened with 'Patience,' transferred

tones of Venetian red. No painted act-drop is used, but a curtain of creamy satin, quilted, having a fringe at the bottom and a valance of embroidery of the character of Spanish work, keeps up the consistency of the colour scheme. This curtain is arranged to drape from the centre. The stalls are covered with blue plush of an inky hue, and the balcony seats are of stamped velvet of the same tint, while the curtains of the boxes are of yellowish silk, brocaded with a pattern of decorative flowers in broken colour.

To turn to a very different subject. I believe a fertile source of annoyance to the public to be the demanding or expecting of fees and gratuities by attendants. This system will, therefore, be discountenanced. Programmes will be furnished and wraps and umbrellas taken charge of gratuitously. The attendants will be paid fair wages, and any attendant detected in accepting money from visitors will be instantly dismissed. I trust that the public will co-operate with me to support this reform (which already works so well at the Gaiety Theatre) by not tempting the attendants by the offer of gratuities. The showing-in of visitors and selling programmes will, therefore, not be sublet to a contractor, who has to pay the manager a high rental, to recoup which he is obliged to extract by his *employés* all he can get out of the public; nor will the refreshment saloons be sublet, but they will be under the supervision of a salaried manager, and the most careful attention will be given to procuring everything of the very best quality.

The theatre will be opened under my management on Monday next, October 10, and I have the satisfaction to be able to announce that the opening piece will be Messrs. W. S. Gilbert and Arthur Sullivan's operá, *Patience*, which, produced at the Opera Comique on April 23, is still running with a success beyond any precedent.

The piece is mounted afresh with new scenery, costumes, and increased chorus. It is being again rehearsed under the personal direction of the author and composer, and on the opening night the opera will be conducted by the composer.

I am, ladies and gentlemen, your obedient servant,

R. D'OYLY CARTE,

BEAUFORT HOUSE, STRAND:
  October 6, 1881,

from the Opera Comique, which was destined to enjoy a fresh lease of popularity.

DETAILS OF CONSTRUCTION

This new theatre has been erected for Mr. D'Oyly Carte from the designs and under the superintendence of Mr. C. J. Phipps, F.S.A., architect of the Gaiety, the Haymarket, the Princess's, and other theatres. It is situate on the west side of Beaufort Buildings, Strand, and occupies a site absolutely isolated on all four sides, thus affording free and expeditious entrance and exit for all classes of the public. The entrances are thus distributed, and are arranged so as to utilise the peculiar levels of the site: For the stalls and dress circle, and for all persons coming in carriages, the entrances are from Somerset Street, just off the Thames Embankment. The pit is also entered here, and there is an entrance to the upper circle. The audience for both these latter parts can come direct from the Strand by a short flight of steps adjoining Beaufort House. In Beaufort Buildings also is an entrance to, and on a level with, the upper circle. The entrances before referred to, from the Embankment, are on a level with the dress circle, and a few steps lead down to the stalls and pit. The gallery is entered from Carting Lane, a street in a direct line from the Embankment to the Strand. The royal entrance is at the angle of Somerset Street and Carting Lane. The stage entrance is in Herbert's Passage, and the box office for booking seats during the day is situated close to the Strand at the angle of the Beaufort Buildings frontage. The theatre is entered from Somerset Street through a semicircular vestibule paved with black and white marble, in which are the offices for booking and obtaining seats in the evening. Doorways immediately opposite the entrances lead to the dress-circle corridor, out of which wide staircases will be found on both sides of the theatre leading to the stalls. From this vestibule are also means of communicating, by an ascending staircase, with the upper circle, and by pass-doors to the pit staircase. All the entrances, passages, and staircases are of fire-resisting material; the flights of stairs are supported at each end by solid brick walls, and each staircase has a hand-rail on either side. There is no part of the theatre that has not two means of both ingress and egress, and the stage is separated from the auditory by a solid brick wall taken up completely through the roof. Water laid on from the high-pressure mains is in several parts of the

The *coup d'œil*, indeed, of a Savoy scene is always amazingly brilliant without being dazzling, as happens theatre, and every possible means has been taken to ensure both comfort and safety to the audience. On the floor below the vestibule is a large refreshment saloon for the pit, and contiguous to it a smoking room opening out of the stalls corridor, with a separate boudoir lounge for ladies. There are also refreshment saloons on the upper floors of the theatre for both the upper circle and gallery, with all necessary retiring and cloak rooms. The auditory is thus arranged: On either side of the stage opening (which is 30 feet wide and 32 feet high) are three private boxes on each of the three levels. These are divided by partitions and ornamental pillars, and are surmounted by an arch spanning the whole width of the proscenium, springing from a cornice on the level of the gallery front. These boxes are richly upholstered in hangings of gold-coloured brocaded silk. The orchestra is in front of the stage, and is of sufficient capacity for a full band of twenty-seven or more musicians. There are nine rows of stalls immediately adjoining the orchestra, seated to hold 150 persons in arm-chairs, with ample space allowed for passing between the several rows, and wide unimpeded gangways on either side of the entrance passages. Behind the stalls are six rows of pit seats, calculated to seat 250 persons, with a spacious open corridor behind for standing and promenading. Above the pit, but at sufficient height to allow of persons at the very back seeing the full height of the scenery, is the dress circle of six rows of seats, with arm-chairs for 160 persons. There are no pillars of any kind in the dress circle, so a clear, unobstructed view of the stage is obtained from every seat. Above the dress circle, but receding some 9 feet back from it, is the upper circle, seated to accommodate 160 persons in five rows. The amphitheatre and gallery recede 5 feet behind the upper circle, and will seat 400 to 500 persons in eight rows. The whole seating accommodation will be for 1,292 persons. In each tier the balcony front takes the form of a horseshoe, that being the best adapted for perfect sight of the stage. The ornamentation of these several balcony fronts is Renaissance in character, and is elaborately moulded and enriched with the figures and foliage peculiar to the Italian phase of the style, and gilded. The ceiling over the auditory takes the form of an extended fan from the arch spanning the proscenium, and is divided into a series of geometric panels, richly modelled in Renaissance ornament in relief, of the same character as

so often when the limelight is profusely used. As
we have seen, the Savoy was one of the first theatres—

the balcony fronts. Colour is sparingly used in the ceiling, the background of the ornament only being painted a light gold colour. The
proscenium arch is divided by ribs and cross-styles into a series of panels,
and the ornament in these is gilded. Over the proscenium in the
tympanum of the arch is a *basso relievo* of figures and foliated ornament. The walls of the auditory are hung with a rich embossed paper,
in two tones of deep Venetian red. The seats are covered in peacock
blue, plush being used for the stalls and stamped velvet for the dress
circle. A pale-gold coloured satin curtain, with an embroidered valance,
takes the place of the usual painted act-drop. The stage, which is laid
with all the latest improvements in mechanical contrivances, is 60 feet
wide, by a depth from the float-light to the back wall of 52 feet. There
is a clear height above the stage of 56 feet for the working of the
scenery, and a sink below of 15 feet. Behind the stage, and occupying
the whole wing of the building in Herbert's Passage, are the dressing-
rooms. The theatre is fitted with a complete system of gas-lighting,
but this is only for use in case of emergency, the whole of the illumi-
nating for all parts of the establishment being by means of electricity.
This has been undertaken by Messrs. Siemens & Co., and the lights
adopted are those introduced by Swan, of Newcastle, and known as the
Swan incandescent light, the power necessary to generate the electric
current for so many lights being supplied by powerful steam-engines
placed in a separate building on the vacant land adjoining the theatre.
These 'Swan' lights are of a beautiful colour, and in no way impair the
atmosphere of the theatre, and emit no heat. They are not of the
piercing brightness of the electric arc lights as seen in our streets and
elsewhere, and therefore not unpleasant to the eyes. This is the first
instance of a public building being lighted permanently in all its departments by the electric light. The exterior façade of the theatre is in
Somerset Street, facing the Thames Embankment, and both this and
the Beaufort Buildings frontage are built of red brick, with Portland
stone for all moulded parts, and are of the Italian style of architecture.
The contractors who have been engaged upon the works are as follows:
Patman & Fotheringham for the whole of the builder's work, including
the stage. Collinson & Lock have arranged the scheme of colour for
the interior, and have executed the painting, papering, and gilding, and

if not the first—at which the electric light was scientifically and elaborately 'laid on,' not merely 'in front of the house,' but behind the scenes. No one who has not seen it can conceive how elaborate and complicated is the mechanism for the control of the lighting. It is admittedly an enormous gain, and possibly a saving in expense, for during the many years of its existence the rich colouring of the *salle* has had to be renewed, I believe, only once—in fact, at this moment it has all the air of a new theatre. The interior is fresh and elegant, the decoration being in white and gold, and set off by crimson draperies. The brocade curtains of a rich mellow tint, which drop from the sides at the close of an act, 'cost a fortune,' as it is called, but have added prodigiously to the general effect.[1]

have supplied the upholstery and carpets; they have also executed the plaster ornamentation of the auditory, in conjunction with Jackson & Sons. Strode & Co. have done the whole of the gas arrangements. Wadman has manufactured the arm-chairs for dress circle and stalls. Burke & Co. have laid down the marble floor of the vestibule. C. Drake & Co. have executed the concrete floors and staircases. Faraday & Son have made all the internal fittings in connection with the electric lighting. Merryweather & Sons have supplied the fire hydrants and other such appliances. Clarke & Co. have constructed the revolving iron shutters and blinds at entrances. Mr. J. E. Walker has been the architect's clerk of works.

[1] There have been many statements and rumours as to the enormous profits made by the partners by these operas. One of the persons most nearly concerned in the venture has given me his views on this subject:

I do not think any regular amount per annum could be reckoned, as, of course, such amounts must vary *enormously* according to the successes

Another of the manager's most important reforms was the introduction of the *queue*, which English play-

of the opera being played. During the first three months of the run of even the most successful opera the receipts are usually almost entirely occupied in paying the current expenses, and the preliminary expenses of production. It is only during the second quarter, and possibly the third quarter, that money as a rule can be made; and the fag end of any piece must always mean a considerable loss, however successful the piece. It may, however, certainly be said of the author and composer in question that not a single one of their joint works in London has been otherwise than *successful*, though the amount of success has of course varied. None of them have been financial losses; all have been financial successes; and this, of course, is a very rare thing with operas.

'The *current* expenses of a Savoy Opera would be somewhere about 130*l*. or 135*l*. a night. The theatre, if perfectly full in every part, would hold about double this. Of course, the expenses I mention are without what I would call the *preliminary* expenses, which, with such an opera as the present, amount to seven or eight thousand pounds; and, therefore, even reckoning on the theatre being full, it is a long time before any money can be made with an opera. In fact, opera, I suppose, in the long run is quite certain to ruin any manager or his backers; with the one exception, of course, of the series of Gilbert and Sullivan operas, which, as I said before, have been an entire exception to the usual rule. The failure of an opera in London, when it has been a very expensive production, and when the period of rehearsals is reckoned, and the period during which the theatre has to be kept open (or, at any rate, rent and many expenses paid) at a loss, would mean a loss anyway of from fifteen to twenty thousand pounds; whereas, of course, a manager would think himself very lucky if out of a successful opera he made seven or eight thousand pounds. I roughly reckon always that ONE ordinary opera FAILURE would swallow up the results of THREE ordinary SUCCESSES. It is of course, therefore, obvious that the whole business must be an exceptionally risky one; and, in fact, in the long run almost a certain loss. It is only where, as with the Gilbert and Sullivan series, you can have a certain success each time, even though it may not always be an *enormous* financial success, that you can look on opera as at all a safe experiment.

goers have always seemed too sturdily independent to adopt. D'Oyly Carte, however, has actually succeeded in inducing his patrons to submit to this custom, to enforce it on themselves, and the pittite may be seen every night falling decorously into line on the flight of steps that descends from the Strand into the Savoy. He was assured at first, with much shaking of heads, that 'they would never stand it.' This sensible arrangement has since been accepted in the case of most theatres in crowded thoroughfares such as the Strand, where the playgoers submit to be marshalled in line by the police, to the great convenience of the passers-by, no longer compelled to make a circuit into the road round the compact crowd.

It may be imagined that the recruiting of the

'I do not think the great or unusual point about the series of Gilbert and Sullivan operas is so much the question of any immense profits made out of them, as that it is (in my opinion) a unique fact that there should be *a series of operas none of which are failures.* So far as enormous profits are concerned, I have no doubt that a little farcical comedy could entirely beat the record of a Gilbert and Sullivan opera, for the reason that the expenses are so entirely out of proportion. I do not know, of course, what has been made by *Charley's Aunt*, for instance, but I should imagine it might probably be equal to what might be made out of eight or ten successful operas, because of the enormous difference in the expenses of the production and the running; but what *is* unique about our operas is that each one has been a success of some sort, and that is what has enabled them to be a permanent business matter. I do not know of any other series of operas that have been. Of course, Italian opera is only kept going regularly by a subscription. Without that it would fall to the ground.'

various travelling corps,[1] usually conducted at the
Savoy itself, involves a good deal of thought, time, and
trouble. There is a perpetual stream of candidates for
the chorus or leading parts, and everyone receives a
fair trial, exhibiting their gifts to Mr. Cellier, the conductor. Often 'blanks are drawn,' and, as may be
imagined, not very often a prize. Many women—a
distressed clergyman's daughter, a child of some family
'reduced'—have found a refuge at the Savoy. Some
friend has promised to 'speak to D'Oyly Carte.' A
regular register of applicants has been kept from the
beginning, with the original notes, of a brief but significant kind; and there are some mystic letters opposite
each; such as 'N.G.,' 'M.,' and 'F.,' which we might
expound as 'No good,' 'Middling,' and 'Fair'; 'Ancient
German' is not so intelligible.[2]

---

[1] This matter of travelling companies has become quite a distinct
business, and few can conceive the importance to which it has grown.
Sunday being a free day, is usually selected as the travelling day, and
some of the great Midland lines are quite in a bustle and ferment from
the abundance of the theatrical specials. Through the great central
stations long trains pass swiftly, Mr. So-and-So's *Jim the Penman's*, or
Uncle Tom's Cabin's performers on board, with all the actors and
actresses, scene-men, 'properties,' and dresses. The Savoy Opera has become a very important commercial enterprise, involving the interests of
a vast number of persons engaged either at the parent theatre or promenading the country. A single travelling company is usually found
sufficient to engross all the energies of a manager; but here the
interests of some seventy or eighty persons, who have to be moved about
the country, become a very serious question.

[2] These details are from an 'At Home' in the *World*, December 4,
1889.

In these opening days of the new house the manager was assisted by a clever man, who had much of the necessary *suaviter in modo* combined with efficiency *in re*—the genial Michael Gunn. He had long been the soul of theatrical enterprise in Dublin, and with the aid of his wife, erst Miss Sudlow, had established the Gaiety Theatre in that city, to which during a long course of years he has brought every shape of peripatetic talent. As a coadjutor to the manager he was invaluable, and at this time directed the numerous travelling companies which were carrying Gilbert and Sullivan ideas all over the land, and 'spreading the light' generally. Everybody in the profession knows Michael Gunn.[1]

It was fortunate for the public stock of harmless pleasure that this co-partnership was established. Nothing could have been happier than the fortuitous concurrence of such elements. Each was exactly what was to be desired for the combination. Gilbert brought his careful diligence, his long training and knowledge of the

---

[1] On one occasion, during a visit to America, he was trying the voices of some candidates for the chorus; one of them sang in a sort of affected Italian-broken-English, which, as Grossmith says, he has 'found quite common among *English foreign singers*.' The stage manager interrupted. 'Look here,' he said, 'that accent won't do for sailors or pirates. Give us a little less Mediterranean, and a little more Whitechapel.' Here Gunn turned and said, 'Of what nationality are you? You don't sound Italian.' The other suddenly dropped his Italian accent, and in Irish brogue said, 'Shure, Mister Gunn, I'm from the same country as yourself.'

stage, with an original method of his own, which was likely to attract the public; Sullivan was the most popular of English composers, with a fertile, unexpected vein of dramatic talent; while D'Oyly Carte, the manager, supplied knowledge of the public taste, joined with business habits. He had the proper managerial spirit of adventure, sparing nothing to produce a good entertainment, with a shrewd deliberation which guarded him from serious risk. The fruit of this alliance was found in some fifteen or sixteen years of almost uninterrupted success, and, given such conditions, the same result may be always assured.

Though the partners were three, the spirit of the undertaking was one, and their co-operation was one. This made the result totally different from what attends the commonly accepted form of procedure. There the story-teller fashions his story and takes it to the composer, who will 'set' it as he will set anything else; just as Swift, it was said, could 'write beautifully on a broomstick'; or it may be that the composer, in want of a story, and wishing 'to write something,' secures a libretto that he thinks will suit. The manager then arrives, and will 'mount' it, just as he will mount anything that will suit his theatre, actors, and singers. Each, therefore, may be considered as working independently and in his own department. The great composers, such as Beethoven, Wagner, or Meyerbeer,

might, indeed, be said to have written their own
librettos; for they composed their works almost before
the story was supplied—that is to say, they had some
favourite story in their minds which filled and inspired
them, and which, as they dwelt on it, found expression
in 'motives,' or a general strain of music. This they
adapted to the words and verses. They saw the great
situations before them, and felt in anticipation how they
should be treated. They would tell their librettist what
they wanted in such a place. Such was Meyerbeer's
method, who almost wrote or rewrote his opera in the
theatre as it was being rehearsed. And so Gilbert, while
giving due point to his lyrics and dialogues, wrote with
a view to what his colleague would make of them, while
the latter bore in mind that he was to accompany, as it
were, and set off the pleasant conceits of his friend.
Both had in view the interests of their manager, the
groupings, scenes, &c.—above all, that original form of
chorus which should exhibit something new on each
occasion. The strangest thing in this association is
that Gilbert has frankly confessed that 'he has no ear
for music. He is very fond of it, but he would hardly
be conscious of a discord. Time and rhythm he
knows.' [1]

---

[1] This suggests an eminent mathematician and chemist whom I knew,
who was utterly impervious to the significance of musical sounds. It
was thus that the mystic, impressive words, ' *Macmillan's Magazine,*'

The *ensemble* suggested by the term 'Savoy Opera' is really of a unique and unusual kind. There is the elegant theatre—almost perfect in its arrangement and sumptuous adornments—the scenery and dresses, on which literally nothing is spared; there is a general magnificence and brilliancy, tempered, however, by good taste and restraint. The choruses are formed of refined and mostly pretty girls, drawn from the 'lower middle classes,' and of a very different type from that found in the common *opera bouffe* chorus. This lends a grace and charm to all that they do. The orchestra is full and rich, and homogeneous from playing together so many years under the same conductor. It might be said, indeed, that it is a little too full and strident for the size of the theatre. *Pianissimos* might be tried occasionally with good effect. There is an admirable and most competent manager, who shrinks from no outlay that he thinks necessary, and who has created quite a gigantic system, spread over the whole kingdom, for the purpose of developing and maturing a school of singers and actors, who are trained and practised, according to their degree, in the country,

conveyed ' no manner of an idea ' to Cardinal Newman's mind. Once a tune played before the mathematician seemed to please, and he said it somehow suggested *chloride of lime*. Yet he had mastered the science of music, and could actually 'score' a piece. Gilbert, I fancy, with practice has learned the comparative value, and suitability to his words, of the different airs.

to be gradually promoted to the London stage. His labours appear unobtrusive, and are felt rather than seen.

Thus, what really distinguishes the Savoy opera from the other kinds of opera is the pervading influence of the author and the composer, which is exerted and felt in every department—in the scenery, dresses, singing, acting, and business. It is all 'Gilbert and Sullivan.' Here the writer can carry out his intentions and meaning so completely that he may be said to act the piece by deputy. The actors and actresses become his second self; every inflection, every movement is his. That curious half-earnest tone in which some grotesque sentiment is gravely uttered, so that we are for a moment in doubt whether the speech is intended seriously, is his; and the actors have caught the style perfectly. At home he has his model theatre, made to scale, and with little blocks to denote groups, &c. He devises all his combinations and entries. This gives a unity to the whole, and it is quite legitimate; for in most cases a writer sees before him the whole incident, as it is in action, to which his words are introductory, but cannot infuse his own ideas into the actors who deliver his words. He, indeed, does not know how to do so. But he feels that his meaning has not been carried out.

'It was in the "Princess,"' said a writer in the *World*
some thirteen years ago, ' that he first displayed on the
stage that ironically comic vein perceptible among the
broader fun of the "Bab Ballads." The leading motive
of the ironical comedy must be sought in the idea that
it is much more comical to bring an apparently serious
personage on the stage and to make him utter the most
bizarre and extravagant sentiments than to produce him
at once in the exaggerated "make-up" beloved of low
comedians. That a comically made-up judge, with a great
red nose and "pantomime" wig and robes, should appear
on the stage and do ridiculous things is only natural.
. . . But it is different when the judge has nothing
unnatural in his appearance, and yet utters the drollest
sentiments. To the fun of the situation and language
is added the important element of surprise. . . . In the
beginning Mr. Gilbert's new theory of fun met with but
scant appreciation among those selected to interpret it.
The reason of this difficulty is obvious. It had become
almost a stage tradition that the actor was at once to
take the audience into his confidence. If a low comedian,
it was expected of him, it was supposed, by his peculiar
audience; and his individuality, as evinced by well-known
tricks and gestures, also went, as he thought, for a great
deal. At least, they secured his "laughs." Mr. Gilbert
found himself obliged to stem this tide of opinion as

best he might. For the purpose of the ironical comedy it was, above all things, necessary that the actor should appear unconscious that what he was saying or doing was funny. He was to play his part in good faith, and let the amusement of the audience arise from the incongruity between his manner and appearance and his acts, words, and deeds. In " Pygmalion " Mrs. Kendal seized the idea perfectly, as did the young lady who played the Scotch lassie in " Engaged," and Miss Marion Terry when she ate the tarts in the same amusing play. It is, perhaps, not easy to utter the oddest lines without betraying some consciousness of their strangeness; but the inventor of this method has succeeded in many cases in getting his intention fairly carried out. There is, and has been for some time past at least, no opposition to his view from the artists who represent his pieces.'

Our author has candidly explained what are his methods of workmanship. No man could be more conscientious or painstaking in providing what he intends shall be worthy of attention; and it is astonishing to find what labour and even drudgery he bestows upon works the superficial might fancy were thrown off in the most airy and careless way. Thus we are told: ' No brilliancy of dialogue, no skilful elaboration of character, will supply the want of a story, serious or comic, as the case may be. Convinced of this, Gilbert lets his story be moulded in the odd hours of the day or night, until it becomes coherent. Then the prosy part of the work commences. First of all he writes the plot out as if it were an anecdote. This covers a few quarto slips of copy, and is written very neatly, almost without correction, so perfectly are the main lines settled before anything is set down. The next proceeding is the more laborious one of expanding the anecdote to the length of an ordinary magazine article by the addition of incident and of summaries of conversations. This being carefully overhauled, corrected, and cut down to a skeleton, the work has taken its third form, and is ready to be broken up into acts; and the scenes, entrances, and exits are arranged. Not till its fifth appearance in manuscript is the play illustrated by dialogue. The important scenes are first written, and then these brightly-coloured patches are gradually knitted together, as it were, by the shorter scenes. At this stage the work is ready for Mr. Sullivan's collaboration, and all begins over again. A song, on which Mr. Gilbert has expended some labour, may happen to be in a metre too nearly resembling one which Mr. Sullivan has previously " set," and must therefore be rewritten. Again, the composer has his ideas as to the order of chorus, song, and duet, and wishes that at some juncture a sentimental air could be grafted on the comic stock. Mr. Sullivan is so sound a musician that he loves to introduce at least one serious air, such

I

as the charming madrigal in the "Pirates of Penzance," which is here the great musical success of the piece, while in America its presence was resented as "out of place in a comic opera." '

Gilbert was once asked by an 'interviewer' where he got his plots, and answered vivaciously: 'Plots? good gracious! where *do* they come from? *I* don't know. A chance remark in conversation, a little accidental incident, a trifling object may suggest a train of thought which develops into a startling plot. Taking my own plots, for instance, the "Mikado" was suggested by a Japanese sword which hangs in my study; the "Yeomen of the Guard" by even a more unlikely incident. I had twenty minutes one day to wait at Uxbridge Station for a train, and I saw the advertisement of the "Tower Furnishing Company," representing a number of beefeaters—why, goodness only knows. It gave me an idea, and I wrote the play originally as one of modern life in the Tower of London.' Everyone with experience of writing knows how true all this is. A trifle suggests something; instantly a whole train of ideas develops, or shows possibilities of development; forms, colours, texture, present themselves. On the other hand, when a fully-formed plot or sequence of incidents is suggested or devised it often seems cold and lifeless, and without form or colour.

The next point is to invent original characters. But

this is a very difficult matter, whether one be writing for
a stock company or writing irrespective of the cast. 'It
is not always easier to write for a non-existent company; one has too free a hand. But with a stock company it is so hard to make the characters seem original.
Writing for the Savoy I had to keep the idiosyncrasies of
Rutland Barrington, Rosina Brandram, and the others
constantly before me. I used to invent a perfectly fresh
character each time for George Grossmith; but he always
did it in his own way—most excellent in itself, crisp and
smart, but "G. G." to the end. Consequently everyone
said: "Why, Grossmith always has the same character";
whereas, if different individuals had acted them, each
would have been distinctive. It was no fault of Grossmith's, than whom a more amiable and zealous *collaborateur* does not exist. It arose from the fact that
his individuality was too strong to be concealed.'

Gilbert once remarked to me that, however well
conceived the character might be, he could not reckon
with any certainty on its 'coming out' as he intended
it. No amount of teaching will ensure that an actor
shall take the author's view. On the other hand, the
actor will often come to the writer's aid, and make a
character out of a mere sketch or indication.

'I write out the play as a story, just as though and
as carefully as though it were to be published in that
form. I then try to divide it into acts. I think two

acts the right number for comic opera. At least, my experience—and that is thirty years old—teaches me so. Sometimes, of course, the original story does not fall readily into two acts, and so requires modification. I put it by for a fortnight or more, and then rewrite the whole thing without referring to the first copy. I find that I have omitted some good things that were in the first edition, and have introduced some other good things that were not in it. I compare the two, put them both aside, and write it out again. Sometimes I do this a dozen times; indeed, the general public have no idea of the trouble it takes to produce a play that seems to run so smoothly and so naturally. One must work up to " a good curtain." '

When the piece is thus written and composed, Gilbert appears in quite another character, as a scene-painter or stage-carpenter. He plots out whole scenes, and models them so exactly that no scope is left for the imagination or the blundering of the workman. Before ' H.M.S. Pinafore ' appeared the author went down to Portsmouth, was rowed about the harbour, viewed various ships, and finally pitched upon the quarter-deck of the ' Victory ' for his scene. Having obtained permission, he sketched and modelled every detail, even to the stanchions. This matter of the scenery is a serious one. It must be pretty and attractive; but not so cumbrous that, like delicate wine, it ' will not travel.' When a comic opera is intended to be played by three companies in England and four in the United States it must be endowed with scenery which will bear carrying from place to place, and will look well in any theatre. Gilbert also designs most of the costumes worn in his plays. This work was not necessary for the ladies' dresses in the ' Pirates of Penzance,' as they are strictly modern ; but when producing the piece in America there was no little difficulty in getting the dress of an English major-general.

Play, scenery, and costumes being arranged, and actors and actresses regularly fitted with parts adapted to their various capacities, next comes the difficulty of stage management. Mr. Gilbert's views on this subject are as autocratic as those of M. Victorien Sardou or Mr. Dion Boucicault ; and by dint of insistence he has acquired as much influence over any company entrusted with his play as even the last-named gentleman, who, in his triple character of manager, author, and actor, may not be said nay to by the most obdurate of low comedians. Mr. Gilbert holds that he is most vitally concerned ; for if the piece succeeds, the whole company and establishment succeed ; but if it fails, it is ' Gilbert's piece ' that has failed, and not its representatives. Hence he insists, except in the case of artists of high rank in their profession, that the characters shall be played according to his own idea. On the rank and file he imposes his commands, and drills them with marvellous patience. Not only at the theatre at set rehearsals, but at his own house, he devotes hour after hour to ' going through the part' with dense but docile artists —' willing, yet slow, to learn.'

Resuming his story, our author explains that ' sometimes, but very rarely, the play is spoilt by the interpreters. They always do their best, but occasionally they fail to realise my intention. The fact is that for comic opera many artists, especially tenors and sopranos, are necessarily engaged who are singers rather than actors ; and it is not to be expected that carefully written comedy dialogue will receive full justice at their hands. It is as though one called on the Haymarket company to perform an opera. Critics do not seem to realise this difficulty, and frequently pronounce a scene to be dull because it is ineffectively acted by a couple of mere concert-singers.

' I next sketch out quite roughly the dialogue, and then fill in the musical numbers as I feel inclined. I do not attempt to write them in order, but just as the humour takes me—one here, one there ; a sad one when I feel depressed, a bright one when I am in a happy mood. When at last all those of the first act are done it is sent to the composer to be set to music, with a copy of the rough sketch of the dialogue to show him how the different songs hang together. I generally like reading it over to the composer, so as to give him my idea of the rhythm, which, as a matter of course, he varies at his pleasure. There must be perfect good-fellowship between the writer and composer, as there is much give-and-take to be managed. Metres have to be changed by the writer, or tunes altered by the composer, to fit in with some idea, some intention, of the other partner. For instance, the writer may have put a theme in one metre and the composer has a tune in his head which will just suit the theme but will not fit the scansion, and so the lyrics must be altered; each must try to make the other's part as easy as possible. There must be no jealousy, no bad feeling between the two. They must be on the best of terms; otherwise there will be no success. And I put down the popularity of the "Gondoliers," "Iolanthe," "Mikado," and the other operas which Sir Arthur Sullivan and I did together chiefly to this fact. He was most kind in this respect.[1]

---

[1] Collaboration is an interesting topic, dramatic almost in its bearing, and its true principles are perhaps little understood. In the case of librettist and composer, the hackneyed or accepted method is for the first to supply a 'book,' which the latter proceeds to set. A genuine composer, however, virtually writes his own play—that is to say, he 'fancies' a subject like *Faust*; as he thinks over the garden scene, the scenes in the cathedral, peculiar tones of music visit him; the whole cast of the strains fill his mind; he feels how he would treat the situations. As he thinks of Margaret's desertion special tones and melodies fill his soul. This was certainly Meyerbeer's, Gounod's, and Wagner's method. The vulgar idea of co-operation in literary work—say a novel—is that one writer shall 'do' the plot, the other the dialogue; or that one shall do one

Well, whilst the composing is going on I complete the dialogue and work up the entire stage management on a model stage. When the rehearsal comes I have the business of each scene written down, and this inspires confidence in those one is teaching; they know that I have a concrete scheme in my head, and generally watch its development with interest and curiosity.

'As to rehearsals, there are in all three weeks for the artistes to study the music; then a fortnight's rehearsals without the music; finally, another three or four weeks' rehearsals in position and with the music. The principals are not wearied with rehearsals until the chorus are perfect in their music.'

This is all interesting, and furnishes a very clear explanation of the Savoy methods.

It has been said—foolishly, it seems to me—that genius is nothing but an unlimited capacity for taking pains; it might run that without taking pains genius will do little. Selection, rejection, arrangement, cumulation, contrast—these things are absolutely necessary to set off genius; but they entail serious labour and take time. Everything can be made the most of and set in the best light provided trouble be taken and

scene, the other another. But real co-operation signifies that *every* portion is done by both—that is, the situations are called over and settled, or amended; the dialogue written by one is taken in hand by the other, altered and enriched, or rewritten.

labour given. Notwithstanding this long course of un-interrupted success, we find our author never relaxing—not, as so many would be tempted to do, 'dashing it off' carelessly and depending on the immunity accorded to an old favourite. But this is not Gilbert's fashion.[1] I found our author lately getting ready a new opera, laying down the keel, timbers, &c., in the most painstaking way. There was a new and stout book which was to be the receptacle for ideas, suggestions, experiments, sketches even. It was already full enough, having rhymeless stanzas later to be fashioned and polished. When the story had been 'blocked out' in the fashion described above, or settled with his coadjutor, they would next fix the likeliest places for the *musical* incidents, the duos, solos, &c. When these were accepted by the composer, the author would proceed at once to write the stanzas, without having touched the dialogue. These the composer would proceed to set, while the librettist got ready the second act in the same fashion. Thus the work went on and gradually grew.

I should have thought that the fashioning the dialogue first would have been a source of inspiration for the lyrics; but every literary workman has his own methods, and uses those that he finds most serviceable.

---

[1] Some years ago there was an exhibition at the Aquarium of theatrical relics, memorials, 'props.,' &c. Among the classes in the cata-

Sullivan's music is *sui generis*. It has nothing in common with the sweet prettiness of the average French light opera; it is more robust and downright, as it were. The French *motifs* seem to depend a good deal on their ingenious and somewhat luscious harmonies; the Sullivan airs are fresh and honest tunes that can be carried in the memory. His style, however, has changed a good deal with his successive operas, and to some extent reflects the taste of the moment; but it is always manly and straightforward. Thus his early works had something of Offenbach, whose exuberant vitality and variety is quite a different thing from the rather sickly sentiment of his successors. 'H.M.S. Pinafore' has a good deal of the breezy tone of 'Madame Angot.'

logue was a heading, 'Mr. W. S. Gilbert, his Sentiments.' It seems that he was asked to contribute to the exhibition, which he declined, but instead he sent a characteristic letter, full of good sense: ' I have a strong feeling that, having regard to the nature of his calling, the actor is sufficiently glorified while he lives, and that it is unnecessary to transfer that glorification to his old clothes after his death. . . . A collection of the wigs of distinguished chief justices or the gaiters and shovel-hats of famous archbishops would not draw five pounds.' George Henry Lewes has given utterance to much the same opinion : ' Reduce the actor to his intrinsic value, and then weigh him with the rivals whom he surpasses in reputation and in fortune. Already he gets more fame than he deserves, and we are called upon to weep that he gets no more! During his reign the applause which follows him exceeds in intensity that of all other claimants for public approbation ; so long as he lives he is an object of strong sympathy and interest ; and when he dies he leaves behind him such influence upon his art as his genius may have effected, and a monument to kindle the emulation of succes· sors. Is not that enough ? '

'Patience' is of quite a different *genre* from 'Princess Ida,' being more of a ballad opera. The fashion in which this music is appreciated in the drawing-room is a tribute to its sterling merits, for we do not find detached songs sung by tenors and sopranos so much as scenes and concerted pieces, which seem to bring back recollections of the pleasant humours of the performance. It is always enjoyable to go over the 'score' in this way, when we appear to have Barrington and Grossmith once more before us. And it must be said that the music bears admirably this transference to the piano.

But perhaps the great merit—or greatest of all his merits—is the admirable way in which the composer has set the words allotted to him. This is done in an almost perfect fashion. The average composer will think it enough if he reflect the sentiment or meaning of the situation; this secured, he will develop his own ideas, using the words as a framework for his notes; much as a milliner will consider the human figure a 'block' on which she can fit her dress. But Sullivan looks on the 'lines' as the air which he is to adorn and 'set off'; he makes everything subservient to this. He puts himself in the place of the author. The two natures are so thoroughly consonant, from practice and habit, that they have come to have the same instincts and feelings. Gilbert knows the sort of music he has to expect, and as he writes keeps this in view; while Sullivan can equally anticipate the quaint points and situations he will have to treat.

Our composer's music *wears* well. It does not seem to grow old-fashioned; this is because it is genuine—or rather, perhaps, because it is really ' good ' music.[1]

Though broad and often exuberant, there is nothing vulgar in Sullivan's work—a note so often struck in Offenbach's strains, which are occasionally *canaille* and reeking of the *café chantant*. In Sullivan's most ' free and easy ' passages there is always a classical tone. It will have struck many, too, how original he is in his forms. In his songs there is nothing of the old insipid Balfian measures, the phrases of which balance each other so symmetrically. What, for instance, could be more strikingly grotesque and novel than the odd, abrupt phrases of the Salvationist duet in ' Ruddigore,' which seems to hint at the spasmodic twists and turns of the sectary's nature?

A contrast to these sprightly runnings are the more solemn and pretentious efforts of the composer, such as the ' Martyr of Antioch,' ' Ivanhoe,' and the popular

---

[1] Rossini was asked what kind of music he liked best, and replied that he only knew of one kind of music—viz. good music. There is much truth in this, as every musician will admit, for the merit of all music is quite independent of its forms, be they trivial or otherwise. That admirable *mæstro* used also to add that he ' liked all music, from Bach to Offen-bach.'

'Golden Legend.' These are excellent, scholarly works, but they seem to lack inspiration, and are academical in style and treatment. It may be laid down that every trained musician can write his cantata or oratorio, just as every *littérateur* can write his novel or biography. It is the regular part of the *métier*. I have heard, indeed, of an eminent mathematician who could not 'distinguish an explosion from a symphony,' who actually learned the science, and could write fugues *secundum artem*. Without inspiration these things are mere exercises. 'Ivanhoe' was certainly a ponderous work, more like a vast symphony protracted through several acts than an opera. It was based on a most artificial libretto, which could not have inspired the composer. His strength, it would seem, is not equal to works of *longue haleine*. I believe, indeed, that if he found a two-act story of a legitimate kind, written by a skilled hand specially for the music, he would produce a comic opera that would astonish the empire.

In a Savoy opera there are two scenes for each piece —one for the first act, the other for the second. Mr. Craven is now usually 'loaned' by the Lyceum to supply some of the most beautiful of his designs. There being little or no changes to be effected, they are usually built up in a very permanent way, and the artist has free scope for his ingenuity. Craven was enabled to devise some beautiful atmospheric effects, for which he has a special gift, by the agency not so much of colour as of what are known as ' mediums '—that is to say, the employment of different lights.

What, then, has been the secret of this great and sustained success? I believe it to be owing to some really unique and original methods devised by author and composer, and carried out in the most thorough and consistent fashion. It amounts, in fact, to what is almost an invention. Gilbert devised a system of investing ordinary colloquial phrases that seem almost trifling with a kind of latent ironical humour which is ordinarily thought too delicate and impalpable for the stage. To these utterances he gave an importance and contrast by curious grotesque surroundings; he added the intended emphasis and brought out their proper meaning by assiduous instruction of those to whom they were entrusted, so that he seemed, as it were, to say the things himself. On his part Sullivan contrived a really wonderful method of musical expression, perfectly appropriate to the sense, so as almost to follow the inflections of the voice in common conversation. I venture to say that no one ever before so perfectly conveyed the meaning of a sentence in common talk by the agency of musical tones. As was before shown, the object was not to find words to show off the music, but to supply music that should illustrate the words.

It would seem that our composer, once in possession

of his story and the spirit of the situations, can write off
his music in a very short space of time, first 'scoring'
the pieces for piano and voices, later adding the
orchestral parts. He no doubt notes, as he goes along,
the fitting instrumental effects, the introduction of
particular instruments and passages, which he will later
develop *secundum artem*. In writing a 'grand opera' a
composer, of course, writes directly for his instruments,
which are the essential mediums of expression ; but in a
Savoy opera the words are the chief element, and the
orchestration of less importance. Sometimes I have
thought that the tone of the Savoy orchestra is
rather loud and sustained. Greater effects could certainly be produced if the general tone were kept sub-
dued, and more delicacy of treatment were aimed at. At
times one would think, indeed, that the instruments were
too zealously carrying out the peers' invitation :

> Loudly let the trumpet bray!
>> Tantantara!
> Gaily bang the sounding brasses !
>> Tring!
> Blow the trumpets, bang the brasses !
>> Tantantara! ting! boom!

No one can have an idea of what can be done in this
direction who has not seen what conducting was in the
old Paris Opéra Comique days, when the exquisite
accompaniments of Auber, Harold, Boildieu, and other

masters were given with surpassing grace and delicacy,
and on a comparatively small orchestra.   In this country
we have plenty of 'time-beaters,' as Von Bulow said,
but conducting is a different thing altogether.

The Savoy play-bill is a work of art, and worth
preserving by the collector of such curios, and it
is interesting to turn over the whole series from the
beginning ; they call up in a very potent way the figures
that have flitted across that pleasant scene, supplying
enjoyment in their passage.   As Elia has shown, a play-
bill is a very mystic talisman in this way.   It would
be interesting to trace the curious genesis and development of the play-bill in these modern days, from the old
antediluvian long and fluttering strip of tissue, with its
rich jet characters which came off on the kid glove and
reposed before you on the cushion of the dress circle, to
the little sheet of note-paper whose faint characters can
with difficulty be read.[1]

The Savoy programmes of the last seven or eight years
were in the form of elegant little oblong booklets or
single cards.   In the case of the earlier ones there were

---

[1] I possess a long series covering a span of some five-and-twenty
years, and giving the cast and characters of all the important plays at
the leading theatres. Nothing is more striking than the decorative style
of these bills, which every year seemed to grow more elaborate in their
treatment. The forms, too, were singularly varied, and seemed to be
dictated by the fashion and pressure of the time, and to have some
significant connection with the social habits of the day.

attempts at colour printing, and presenting selected scenes and figures from the more successful of the operas. But it was for the ' Yeomen of the Guard,' I think, that Miss Alice Havers furnished a really elegant design— two quaint figures leaning on an altar, and delicately tinted, which was reproduced by a German firm in sympathetic fashion. This was found so acceptable that it has been retained, with some slight variation, as the standing form of bill. This, no doubt, is a trifling matter, but it contributes something to the sense of enjoyment : it gives pleasure to the eye, and is evidence of the general artistic feeling in other directions.

Grossmith has related the regular course and incidents at the rehearsals at the Savoy. The music is always learned first—the choruses, finales, &c., are composed first in order, then the quartettes and trios, the songs last. Sometimes, owing to changes and rewriting, these are given out to the singers very late. The song in the second act of ' Princess Ida ' was given to Grossmith only a night or two before the performance, and he found his chief difficulty not in learning the new tune, but in un-learning the old one. ' The greatest interest is evinced by us all as the new vocal numbers arrive. Sir A. Sullivan will come suddenly, a batch of manuscript under his arm, and announce that there is something new. He plays over the new number—the vocal parts only are written. The conductor listens and watches, and after

K

hearing them played over a few times contrives to pick up all the harmonies, casual accompaniments, &c.' Sir Arthur is always strict in wishing that his music shall be sung exactly as he has written it. One of the leading performers was singing an air at a rehearsal, not exactly dividing the notes as they were written, and giving the general form, as it were. 'Bravo!' said Sir Arthur, 'that is really a very good air of yours. Now, if you have no objection, I will ask you to sing mine.' This is pleasant.

Gilbert always listens carefully during these recitals, making mental notes for possible effects. At his home, as I have said, he has his little model stage, where the characters are represented by little bricks of various colours, the chorus being distinguished from the lead-ing singers.[1]

In his reminiscences Grossmith supplies many 'good stories' about the chorus One, who assured his friends that he was the coming Sims Reeves, sent this telegram to the manager: 'Suffering from hoarseness, cannot appear to-night.' Another begged of Grossmith to let him come and sing his 'patter song' for him. After the song Grossmith good-naturedly said, 'I suppose you want me to recommend you to Mr. Carte for the chorus?' 'Oh, no,' was the reply; 'Mr. Carte has heard me and

---

[1] No expense is spared to get the requisite accuracy, and I believe the little model of a ship for the late revival of *Pinafore* cost some 60*l*.

says I am not good enough. So I thought you might recommend me to play your parts on tour.' This 'being tried' by Mr. D'Oyly Carte has become a popular resource. Innumerable persons are 'being tried,' or looking forward to being 'tried by D'Oyly Carte.'

As I have stated, many a pleasing girl with a nice voice and of good parentage has found refuge at the Savoy.

There is room for a large number, owing to the many travelling Savoy companies wandering over the kingdom. The manager is always on the watch for anyone that at all 'stands out' in the background, and promotion follows to a small part, or perhaps to London.

Most of the tenors—notably Mr. Pounds—have come from the ranks in this fashion. Some of these are 'born gentlemen,' as it is called, and at this moment the two principal tenors belong to that category. That pleasing and popular *tenorino* George Power was the son of Sir John Power, and associated with the early glories of the 'Sorcerer' and 'Pirates.' Manners, too, was of gentle birth. But the impartial manager will

> Spurn not the nobly born
> With love affected,
> Nor treat with virtuous scorn
> The well-connected.
> High rank involves no shame.

The musical rehearsals, Grossmith tells us, are 'child's play in comparison with the stage rehearsals. Mr. Gilbert is a perfect autocrat, insisting that his words shall be delivered, even to an inflection of the voice, as he dictates. He will stand on the stage beside the actor or actress, and repeat the words, with appropriate action, over and over again until they are delivered as he desires. In some instances, of course, he allows a little licence, but a very little.'

Grossmith then describes a typical scene. Say Mr. Snooks has to utter some such sentence as this : 'The king is in the counting-house.' This is his *whole* part, and he naturally wishes to make it go as far as possible. He accordingly enters with a grotesque, slow walk which he has carefully practised. He is instantly checked by the author. ' Please don't enter like that, Mr. Snooks. We don't want any comic-man business here.' ' I beg pardon, sir,' poor Snooks replies, ' I thought you meant the part to be funny.' ' Yes, so I do, but I don't want you to tell the audience you're the funny man. They'll find it out, if you are, quickly enough.' Snooks tries again, entering with smart rapidity. ' No, no, don't hurry in that way. Enter like this.' And Gilbert showing him the way, the thing is got right at last. He then repeats his line, ' The king is in the counting-house,' laying the accent on *house*. This has to be gone over again and again, but without result. The luckless

player will make it *house*. At last the author gives it
up in despair, and announces that as it would be impossible to cut out the line altogether, which he would gladly
do, he would be obliged reluctantly to allot the character
to someone else. 'Do think a moment,' he says,
'before you speak now.' The wretched man endeavours
to think, and then, quite desperate, almost shouts, 'The
king is in the counting-HOUSE.' 'We won't bother about
it any more,' says Gilbert, 'get on with the next—Grossmith—where's Grossmith?' However, at the end of
the rehearsal our author good-naturedly accosts the
despairing Snooks, and comforts him. 'Don't worry
yourself about that. Go home and think it over. It will
be all right to-morrow.' On the morrow, however, it
is much the same, but by dint of incessant repeating,
like Smike, 'Who calls so loud?' the proper emphasis
is at last secured.

So conscientious are our authors in preparing their
effects that on the rehearsals of the last piece a sort of
stage or scaffold was raised in the stalls to enable them
to have the correct 'audience view' of all that was doing.
At the final full-dress rehearsal the night before the
performance, though the theatre was filled, the first
three rows of the stalls were railed off, so as to allow
composer and writer a free range to study the effects.

The gathering of peers in 'Iolanthe' was one of
the most striking exhibitions we have had on the stage,

owing to the rich gala robes and the quaint, old-fashioned
air of the figures. Here we have one of those unusual
and original ideas of Gilbert's which would not occur
to less practical minds. There is a curious chord
touched, something verging on the solemn even, in this
evoking of the past. When these old costumes are
brought before us, minutely accurate in every detail, a
procession of ghosts seems to pass before us. We have
much the same feeling as we turn over the pictures in
'Pickwick.' In his 'Ages Ago' and in 'Ruddigore'
there is the same effective element.

On this occasion strict old-fashioned shaving was *de
rigueur*, and every peer was to be bald a-top, and display
little or no hair save the correct 'mutton-chop' whisker.
It would have 'arrided' Scarron himself to learn that
the general order for shaving excited strong resistance
in the chorus. It verged on a strike. The excuses
were amusing. One was a traveller in the day-time, and
though a peer by night, he would lose custom by appear-
ing so young. Another was a 'spirit leveller,' and it was
unusual in his calling to be without moustaches. A
third was paying his addresses to a young lady who
would be sure to object. All, however, yielded, save one,
who actually 'resigned.' In the 'Mikado' there was also
a general Japanese shaving, likewise in 'Ruddigore.'

When this latter piece was being prepared, so
conscientious was the presentation that the pictures of

the ancestors were all drawn from individual members, so that the likenesses should be recognised. I doubt, however, if this were noticed, for it is almost a principle of scenic representations that *de minimis non curat audientia*. For scenic effect it is enough to indicate. All, however, had to repair to the photographer's.[1]

One of the many Josephines who figured in the early performances of the 'Pinafore,' Grossmith relates, ' objected to standing anywhere but in the centre of the stage,' assuring Mr. Gilbert that she was accustomed to occupy that position and no other. Mr. Gilbert said, most persuasively, 'Oh, but this is *not* Italian opera; this is only a low burlesque of the worst possible kind.' 'He says this sort of thing in such a quiet and serious way that one scarcely knows whether he is joking or not.'

On another occasion, he called out from the middle of the stalls—his favourite position at rehearsal : 'There is a gentleman in the left group not holding his fan

---

[1] In this connection an amusing incident occurred. The manager, meeting a member of the chorus, asked had he been photographed. ' I go to-morrow,' was the reply; 'you see, sir, I have shaved.' Meeting him again, the manager noticed the moustache, and asked had he been to the photographer's, and was told that he had been there yesterday. A little mystified, he thought he had made a mistake. At the first dress rehearsal the actor was there without moustache; but meeting him the next day, he had one! The actor explained that he had to sing at concerts, that without a moustache the effect would be lost, so he had contrived a false one, which did very well.

correctly.' The stage manager appeared, and explained : 'There is one gentleman who is absent through illness.' 'Ah !' said the author, as gravely as if he were his own pirate captain, 'that is not the gentleman I am referring to.'

And when Grossmith and Miss Jessie Bond were rehearsing the 'Mikado,' the lady was to give him a push, and he was to roll completely over. 'Would you mind omitting that ?' Gilbert asked, with much politeness. 'Certainly, if you wish it,' said the other ; 'but I get an enormous laugh by it.' 'So you would if you sat down on a pork pie,' said the other.[1]

One of the costly burdens laid upon managers, of which the light-hearted audience takes little thought, is the providing of substitutes for the leading performers, in case sickness should hinder the appearance of the principal personage. In the case of actors and actresses the contingency is remote enough, and there is usually sufficient time to find a *remplaçant*, for the performer, though suffering, can struggle through his part for a night or two. But in the case of a singer the interruption is usually of a sudden kind. A cold may at once deprive him of his voice. The 'understudy,' as he is called, is usually one of the smaller characters, whose place, not very important, can be supplied at a

[1] Swift, a great authority, however, declares that the finest pieces of wit will never produce such intense enjoyment or appreciation as the simple results of slyly drawing away a chair when a person is about to sit down.

short notice. He or she thus often gains a favourable opportunity of distinction. There must be something grotesquely humorous in the situation, both parties jealously watching each other, the performer naturally being determined, if he can help it, to furnish no opportunity for a possible rival; the understudy feverishly taking stock of any symptom of failure in his principal. When Grossmith was playing in the ' Sorcerer' one of these ' deputies' was specially retained to supply his place in case of accidents. ' During the first week,' the actor tells us, ' he used to come to me each night and ask how I was. On my replying that I was all right, never better, it appeared to me that he departed with a disappointed look. His kind inquiries were repeated, as I thought, with extra anxiety; but still I kept well, and showed no signs of fatigue. Then he began to insist that I was not looking well, and I replied that, looks or no looks, I was perfectly well. Finally, he came to me with a pill which he was certain would " do " for me.' This is an amusing situation, yet natural withal, akin to that of the physician who is forced to bewail an unhealthy season. In fact, the too healthy Grossmith was destined to play his character two hundred nights without a break, and nearly *seven hundred* of ' Pinafore.' But in the third week of the ' Pirates' Grossmith's father died, and the longed-for opportunity came. The substitute, at almost a moment's notice, had to assume the major-general's part, and did it remarkably well under the circumstances.

Foremost among the attractive girls who have been
enlisted in the chorus, there was one whose refined features and sympathetic grace began early to distinguish
her from her companions. This was ' Miss Fortescue,'
as she was called. The audience could note a curious
earnestness and eagerness to do her duty in the best
way ; there was never any perfunctory execution of her
duties ; she seemed to throw herself into the part, small
as it was. Miss Fortescue had many friends, though
but a simple chorus maiden. But even on the stage it
is always the performer that raises the office, not the
office the performer. No stage is so strictly regulated as
that of the Savoy. No danglers are tolerated behind
the scenes. It is like a family. There is literally ' no
admission except on business.'

An admirer presently appeared, a youth of high
degree—the son of a well-known peer—who was capti-
vated by the charms of the young chorus-singer. The
noble family, as may be imagined, were opposed to this
alliance, as they wished for something more suitable and
of corresponding rank. There was something, too, almost
grotesque in the shock given to their known religious
prejudices by this alliance with a stage-player—the Earl
belonging to the ' unco guid.' It was much to his credit
that, after a short resistance to his son's somewhat
hasty partiality, he gave way, and cordially and honour-
ably received the young man's choice. Had the Earl,

however, had the chance of seeing a little piece written by Andrew Halliday (which was highly unlikely)— the story turned on a similar alliance—he could not have more completely availed himself of the shrewd recipe given by the lord in that drama—which was not to oppose, but to encourage, the folly, and leave the rest to the youth. In time the fickle young man grew tired of his passion, became ' uncertain, coy, and hard to please,' and after some painful episodes the affair was broken off.[1]

Much indignation was felt for the wanton fashion in which the poor girl had been treated. But her friends stood by her gallantly. Mr. Gilbert notably championed her cause ; and when an action at law was proposed, for the purpose of punishing the swain, he took a zealous share in all the discussions, and finally succeeded in obtaining a very substantial pecuniary *amende* from the family—10,000*l*. in short. This sum could hardly be held to indemnify her for the loss of the glittering position which had been promised to her ; but no one wished to gratify the public taste for a *cause célèbre,* or a public representation of the ' Trial by Jury.'

Having always had aspirations for the regular drama, she determined to seize the opportunity for devoting herself entirely to acting. She later formed a

---

[1] I was at the theatre one night, seated in the box next to theirs, just as the business had reached this distressing stage. It was easy to see what was in his thoughts.

company of her own, in which she played the various important heroines. I have seen her perform the somewhat antiquated part of Julia in the ' Hunchback ' with much judicious effect. She has thrown her whole energies into her calling. Such is this little romance of the Savoy.

The original group, consisting of Grossmith, Barrington, Jessie Bond, and Durward Lely, had grown to be completely associated with the Savoy conceptions. They were to the manner born. The public grew accustomed to them, and came to know their ways by heart. No tenor could have been better suited to the office or more acceptable to the audience than Lely. He sang his songs with a pleasing and melodious voice, yet without any of the effusiveness of the operatic tenor. He was the character first; he harmonised admirably with his companions. In the ' Mikado ' he was particularly suited. Later, however, he chose to sever his connection with the theatre and seek a more brilliant fortune on the regular stage. He has lost his regular, sympathetic audience, and has joined the ranks of the innumerable singers who can enjoy but fitful and precarious engagements. Another singer took his place—Courtice Pounds. He came from one of the travelling companies of the Savoy, and had a good voice, though he was somewhat lacking in refinement. He, too, after some years departed for newer and broader musical pastures.

Having thus for a short span lifted a corner of the curtain, we shall now return to the regular course of events. A new opera had been got ready, of a slightly different pattern. Gilbert has a *penchant* for the fairy business, and returns to it when he can. He seems at home in fairyland, though it may be doubted if such subjects and such topics are now ' up to date,' as it is called. Audiences are hardly so confiding as they were in the days of the ' Palace of Truth.' I fancy, however, that ' Creatures of Impulse,' which has enjoyed long popularity, could be fitted to operatic music with great success. The new venture was

Produced at the Savoy Theatre, Saturday, November 25, 1882, under the management of Mr. R. D'Oyly Carte.

IOLANTHE
OR
THE PEER AND THE PERI

Dramatis Personæ

THE LORD CHANCELLOR	MR. GEORGE GROSSMITH
EARL OF MOUNTARARAT	MR. RUTLAND BARRINGTON
EARL TOLLOLLER	MR. DURWARD LELY
PRIVATE WILLIS (*of the Grenadier Guards*) .	MR. CHARLES MANNERS
STREPHON (*an Arcadian Shepherd*) . .	MR. R. TEMPLE
QUEEN OF THE FAIRIES	MISS ALICE BARNETT
IOLANTHE (*a Fairy, Strephon's Mother*) .	MISS JESSIE BOND
CELIA	MISS FORTESCUE
LEILA (*Fairies*) . . .	MISS JULIA GWYNNE
FLETA	MISS SYBIL GREY
PHYLLIS (*an Arcadian Shepherdess and Ward in Chancery*)	MISS LEONORA BRAHAM

Chorus of Dukes, Marquises, Earls, Viscounts, Barons, and Fairies

ACT I.—An Arcadian Landscape

ACT II.—Palace Yard, Westminster

DATE.—BETWEEN 1700 AND 1882

Scenery by Mr. H. Emden. Costumes by Miss Fisher, Messrs. Ede & Sons, Messrs. Frank Smith & Co., Messrs. E. Moses & Son, M. Alias, and Madame Auguste et Cie. Dances arranged by Mr. J. D'Auban. Perruquier, Mr. Clarkson.

Of all the images left by this piece on the memory, that of the wiry, grotesque, sprite-like figure of Grossmith as the Lord Chancellor, frisking about in his gorgeous black and gold robe, is the most piquant and effective. Who will forget his quaint dance and original antics, in which there was nothing vulgar or too extravagant? This functionary wishes to marry Phyllis, a ward of his court, and bewails the embarrassment of his position, which is akin to that of Pooh-Bah in the 'Mikado.' Lord Tolloller says :

My lord, I desire, on the part of this House, to express its sincere sympathy with your lordship's most painful position.

Lord Chan. I thank your lordships. The feelings of a Lord Chancellor who is in love with a ward of court are not to be envied. What is his position? Can he give his own consent to his own marriage with his own ward? Can he marry his own ward without his own consent? And if he marries his own ward without his own consent, can he commit himself for contempt of his own court? And if he commit himself for contempt of his own court, can he appear by counsel before himself, to move for arrest of his own judgment ? Ah, my lords, it is indeed painful to have to sit upon a woolsack which is stuffed with such thorns as these !

This is a favourite topic of our author. One of the wittiest songs in the whole Gilbertian *répertoire* is based on the humorous notion that rank becomes a dis-

THE LORD CHANCELLOR

ability. As we think of ' Blue Blood ' and its Balfian air a smile comes involuntarily to the lips. As verses the strophes are admirable :

CHORUS

Nay, do not shrink from us—we will not hurt you—
The peerage is not destitute of virtue.

BALLAD—LORD TOLLOLLER

Spurn not the nobly born
  With love affected,
Nor treat with virtuous scorn
  The well-connected.
High rank involves no shame—
We boast an equal claim
With him of humble name
  To be respected !
Blue blood ! Blue blood !
  When virtuous love is sought
  Thy power is naught,
Though dating from the flood,
    Blue blood !

    CHORUS. Blue blood ! Blue blood ! &c.

Spare us the bitter pain
  Of stern denials,
Nor with lowborn disdain
  Augment our trials.
Hearts just as pure and fair
May beat in Belgrave Square
As in the lowly air
  Of Seven Dials !
Blue blood ! Blue bood !
  Of what avail art thou
  To serve us now ?
Though dating from the flood,
    Blue blood !
    CHORUS. Blue blood ! Blue blood ! &c.

In this piece Gilbert has laid hands on a prime jest
in the Pickwick trial and developed it :

STREPH. No evidence! You have my word for it. I tell you that she bade me take my love.

STREPHON, MR. TEMPLE

L

Lord Chan. Ah! but, my good sir, you mustn't tell us what she told you—it's not evidence. Now, an affidavit from a thunderstorm, or a few words on oath from a heavy shower, would meet with all the attention they deserve.

His lordship is thus humorously described when on the bench :

His lordship is constitutionally as blithe as a bird—he trills upon the bench like a thing of song and gladness. His series of judgments in F sharp, given *andante* in six-eight time, are among the most remarkable effects ever produced in a Court of Chancery. He is, perhaps, the only living instance of a judge whose decrees have received the honour of a double encore.

Mr. Gilbert occasionally elaborates a conceit in a rather minute and ingenious way. Here we have Strephon, who is ' half a fairy '—that is, ' a fairy down to the waist, but his legs are mortal.' He is also ' inclined to be stout,' but the queen says, ' I see no objection to stoutness, *in moderation* '—a true Gilbertian touch. The hint of the half fairy is worked out with ingenuity :

Leila. Your fairyhood doesn't seem to have done you much good.

Streph. Much good ! It's the curse of my existence ! What's the use of being half a fairy ? My body can creep through a keyhole, but what's the good of that when my legs are left kicking behind ? I can make myself invisible down to the waist, but that's of no use when my legs remain exposed to view. My brain is a fairy brain, but from the waist downwards I'm a gibbering idiot. My upper half is immortal, but my lower half grows older every day, and some day or

other must die of old age. What's to become of my upper
half when I've buried my lower half I really don't know.

PHYLLIS, MISS BRAHAM

QUEEN. I see your difficulty, but with a fairy brain you
should seek an intellectual sphere of action. Let me see.

L 2

I've a borough or two at my disposal. Would you like to go into Parliament?

Iol. A fairy member! That would be delightful!

Streph. I'm afraid I should do no good there. You see, down to the waist I'm a Tory of the most determined descrip-

IOLANTHE, MISS BOND; STREPHON, MR. TEMPLE

tion, but my legs are a couple of confounded Radicals, and on a division they'd be sure to take me into the wrong lobby. You see, they're two to one, which is a strong working majority.

Queen. Don't let that distress you; you shall be returned as a Liberal-Conservative, and your legs shall be our peculiar care.

STREPH. (*bowing*). I see your Majesty does not do things by halves.

QUEEN. No, we are fairies down to the feet.

PRIVATE WILLIS, MR. MANNERS; QUEEN OF THE FAIRIES, MISS BARNETT

This is somewhat artificial, but it is amusing. Further on it recurs again :

Iol. No matter! The Lord Chancellor has no power over you. Remember you are half a fairy. You can defy him—down to the waist.

Streph. Yes, but from the waist downwards he can commit me to prison for years! Of what avail is it that my body is free, if my legs are working out seven years' penal servitude?

Produced at the Savoy Theatre, on Saturday, January 5, 1884, under the management of Mr. R. D'Oyly Carte.

PRINCESS IDA
or
CASTLE ADAMANT
Dramatis Personæ

King Hildebrand	Mr. Rutland Barrington
Hilarion (*his Son*)	Mr. Bracy
Cyril ⎱ (*Hilarion's Friends*) .	Mr. Durward Lely
Florian ⎰	Mr. Charles Ryley
King Gama, ...	Mr. George Grossmith
Arac ⎱	Mr. R. Temple
Guron ⎰ (*his Sons*) . .	Mr. Warwick Grey
Scynthius ⎰	Mr. Lugg
Princess Ida (*Gama's Daughter*) . .	Miss Leonora Braham
Lady Blanche (*Professor of Abstract Science*)	Miss Brandram
Lady Psyche (*Professor of Humanities*) .	Miss Kate Chard
Melissa (*Lady Blanche's Daughter*) .	Miss Jessie Bond
Sacharissa ⎱	Miss Sybil Grey
Chloe ⎰ (*Girl Graduates*) . .	Miss Heathcote
Ada ⎰	Miss Lillian Carr

Soldiers, Courtiers, ' Girl Graduates,' ' Daughters of the Plough,' &c.

ACT I.—Pavilion in King Hildebrand's Palace
ACT II.—Gardens of Castle Adamant
ACT III.—Courtyard of Castle Adamant

'Princess Ida' was perhaps the least interesting of the series. It seemed too poetical, and was, in fact, a sort of adaptation of Tennyson's poem, the 'Princess.'[1] It also might be considered one of the 'Fairy Comedies' set to music. Now, as I have said, the 'Palace of Truth' and the other pieces of its class had a popularity that was a little perplexing; for it seemed phenomenal almost that the delicate conceits of poetry, with declamations in blank verse, should have been so acceptable to mixed audiences who were both highly fashionable and highly vulgar. The same puzzle was offered by the extravagant craze for Mr. Rider Haggard's fictions, 'She' and 'King Solomon's Mines.' The composer eagerly seized the opportunity for music of the more regular operatic pattern. Everyone listened with pleasure to these elaborate strains, and to the themes which were worked out and worked up in masterly fashion. It was, however, a new departure, and this setting was scarcely suited to the Gilbertian conceits, which it almost overpowered. Here is a fair specimen of these three acts of smooth verse :

> *Enter* KING HILDEBRAND, *with* CYRIL
> HILD. See you no sign of Gama ?
> FLOR.   None, my liege !

---

[1] Our author had, in fact, adapted it himself, the piece having already been presented to the public many years before, at the Olympic, as a poetical drama.

HILDEBRAND

It's very odd indeed. If Gama fail
To put in an appearance at our Court
Before the sun has set in yonder west,
And fail to bring the Princess Ida here,
To whom our son Hilarion was betrothed
At the extremely early age of one,
There's war between King Gama and ourselves!
(*Aside to* CYRIL.) Oh, Cyril, how I dread this interview!
It's twenty years since he and I have met.
He was a twisted monster—all awry—
As though Dame Nature, angry with her work,
Had crumpled it in fitful petulance!

Grossmith was here not very well suited, and his King Gama seemed somewhat after the pattern of monarchs in burlesque. The piece was singularly fortunate in the group of the three young nobles, performed by Durward Lely, Bracy, and Ryley. At the present moment it would be difficult to find for a single piece three young men of graceful mien and good figure, with tuneful, cultivated tenor voices, such as this trio possessed. As they scaled the wall of the Girton of fairyland, they sang:

We've learnt that prickly cactus
Has the power to attract us
           When we fall.
ALL.   When we fall!

FLORIAN

That bull-dogs feed on throttles—
That we don't like broken bottles
           On a wall.
ALL.   On a wall!

HILDEBRAND

That spring-guns breathe defiance,
And that burglary's a science
                                        After all.

ALL.   After all !

There is little inspiration in such a situation (it is hard to escape the Gilbertian metre), and it shows how quaintly our author can deal with such a subject. We like the notion of ' Daughters of the Plough ' figuring in the castle, who attend and serve the *al fresco* repast to this cheerful strain :

> Merrily ring the luncheon bell !
> Here, in meadow of Asphodel,
> Feast we body and mind as well ;
> So merrily ring the luncheon bell !

On which their preceptress sings :

> Hunger, I beg to state,
> Is highly indelicate.

When the three 'strong men' are getting ready for battle they intone this strain :

SONG—ARAC

> We are warriors three,
> Sons of Gama, Rex ;
> Like most sons are we,
> Masculine in sex.

ALL THREE

> Yes, yes,
> Masculine in sex.

ARAC

This helmet, I suppose,
Was meant to ward off blows ;
      It's very hot,
      And weighs a lot,
As many a guardsman knows,
So off that helmet goes.

THE THREE KNIGHTS

      Yes, yes,
So off that helmet goes !
      [*Giving their helmets to attendants.*

.   .   .   .   .

ARAC

These things I treat the same
                              [*Indicating leg-pieces.*
(I quite forget their name).
      They turn one's legs
      To cribbage pegs—
Their aid I thus disclaim,
Though I forget their name.

ALL THREE

      Yes, yes,
Though we forget their name,
Their aid we thus disclaim !
They remove their leg-pieces and wear close-fitting shape suits.

It will be noted that 'Princess Ida' is the only one of the
series that is cast in the form of three acts—a shape
which was not altogether to its advantage.   It is curious,
by the way, to note the gradual change that has been made
during the past fifteen or sixteen years or so in the form

and measure of the comic opera. In translations of
the comic opera of the French pattern, three acts
was *de rigueur*, and the piece was always laid out in that
form. Three dramatic situations or exhibitions seemed
necessary for the development. The first was introductory; the second the crisis or complication; the third
the extrication or winding-up. This seemed logical
enough; but the form and pressure of the time, which
dispense with all superfluity, required that the writers
should ' come to the point at once'—to the ' 'osses,' in
fact—and reach the development by the close of the
first act, while the second should contain the solution.
Both systems have their merits, but it must be said that
the older form now seems a little tedious and protracted,
and that there is not enough ' stuff' to cover the canvas.
This question of acts and scenes offers an interesting
subject of speculation, and, like the division of a novel
into chapters, is a point not of form but of substance.
A chapter should be a complete portion of the action,
and represent an episode. Our plays are now invariably
cast in the form of three acts—or scenes, rather—whereas
formerly nothing under five would be tolerated. I fancy
there is a loss of interest by the more rapid development,
as the gradual progress of the five acts fosters a sort of
acquaintance and familiarity with the characters. The
elaborate nature of the set scenes now in fashion
has virtually abolished the succession of scenes in an act,

as it has become impossible to change a scene as a cloth
or ' flats' used to be changed.

Gilbert has been the chief agent in effecting this
alteration, and has really educated his audience into
contentment with two scenes and no more.

If there was found a slight failure of attraction in the
last two operas, the authors were now to rally their
energies with extraordinary success, and, reverting to
their proper methods, to eclipse in brilliancy all previous
efforts. This grand success was

*Produced at the Savoy Theatre, on Saturday, March 14,
1885, under the management of Mr. R. D'Oyly Carte.*

THE MIKADO
OR
THE TOWN OF TITIPU

Dramatis Personæ

THE MIKADO OF JAPAN	MR. R. TEMPLE
NANKI-POO (*his Son, disguised as a wandering minstrel, and in love with Yum-Yum*) .	MR. J. G. ROBERTSON
KO-KO (*Lord High Executioner of Titipu*) .	MR. GEORGE GROSSMITH
POOH-BAH (*Lord High Everything Else*) .	MR. RUTLAND BARRINGTON
GO-TO	MR. R. CUMMINGS
PISH-TUSH (*a noble Lord*)	MR. RUDOLPH LEWIS
YUM-YUM ⎫	MISS GERALDINE ULMAR
PITTI-SING ⎬ (*three Sisters—Wards of Ko-Ko*)	MISS A. COLE
PEEP-BO ⎭	MISS SYBIL GREY
KATISHA (*an elderly Lady, in love with Nanki-Poo*)	MISS ROSINA BRANDRAM

Chorus of School-girls, Nobles, Guards, and Coolies

ACT I.—Courtyard of Ko-Ko's Official Residence
ACT II.—Ko-Ko's Garden

Both scenes painted by Mr. Hawes Craven

Stage Manager . . . . Mr. W. H. Seymour

Every evening at 7.30, the entirely new and original operetta entitled

MRS. JARRAMIE'S GENIE

Words by Frank Desprez. Music by Alfred & François Cellier (Nos. 1 and 2 by François Cellier. Nos. 3, 4, and 5 by Alfred Cellier)

MORTALS

Mr. Harrington Jarramie *(a retired Upholsterer)*	Mr. Wallace Brownlow
Ernest Pepperton	Mr. J. Wilbraham
Smithers *(Butler)*	Mr. Charles Gilbert
Bill ⎫ *(Railway Carmen)* . . . Jim ⎭	⎰ Mr. Lebreton ⎱ Mr. Metcalfe
Mrs. Harrington Jarramie . . .	Miss M. Christo
Daphne *(her Daughter)*	Miss R. Hervey
Nixon *(Parlour-maid)*	Miss M. Russell

IMMORTAL

Ben-Zoh-Leen *(the Slave of the Lamp)* . .	Mr. John Wilkinson

SCENE.—Morning-room, Mr. Jarramie's House, Harley Street, London

The 'Mikado' is certainly the most popular and best known of all these entertainments. This piece and 'Pinafore' are, perhaps, the only ones that have found their way to foreign countries.

I myself have seen at an obscure Dutch town wall-posters, printed in the vernacular, and announcing 'Het Mikado, van Gilbert—Sullivan.' One of Mr. D'Oyly

Carte's travelling companies took it to Berlin and to brilliant Vienna, where dance tunes and Strauss have their home, and where it caused unbounded enjoyment.

The Japanese 'business' naturally offered excellent opportunities for scenery and decoration, contrasting in

MR. ROBERTSON AS NANKI-POO

a striking way with what had hitherto been attempted. The brilliancy and glitter of the colours, with the richness of the materials employed for the dresses, were really exceptional. The gold brocade dresses of the Mikado and his Lord High Executioner might have been worn by Japanese dignitaries of corresponding rank, and cost an

enormous sum. It was reported, indeed, that Japanese
functionaries had been called into council and had given
grave advice on the
scenic arrangements.

The central hu-
morous idea of the
piece turned upon
the situation of
'Pooh-Bah,' a part
discharged with in-
finite grotesqueness
by the ever-facetious
Barrington. The
Lord High Every-
thing Else explains
that when all the
great officers of state
had resigned in a
body because they
were too proud to
serve under an 'ex-
tailor,' he accepted
all their posts at
once. This led to

MR. G. GROSSMITH AS KO-KO

some embarrassment, as when the Lord High Executioner consults him about his approaching marriage
and the sums of money he ought to lay out:

Pooh. In which of my capacities? As First Lord of the Treasury, Lord Chamberlain, Attorney-General, Chancellor of the Exchequer, Privy Purse, or Private Secretary?

MISS BRANDRAM AS KATISHA

Ko. Suppose we say as Private Secretary?

Pooh. Speaking as your Private Secretary, I should say that as the city will have to pay for it, *don't stint yourself, do it well.*

Ko. Exactly—as the city will have to pay for it. That is your advice?

Pooh. As Private Secretary. Of course you will understand that as Chancellor of the Exchequer I am bound to see that due economy is observed.

Ko. Oh, but you said just now, 'Don't stint yourself, do it well.'

Pooh. As Private Secretary.

Ko. And now you say that due economy must be observed.

Pooh. As Chancellor of the Exchequer.

This jest tickled the public hugely.

Ko-Ko, the Lord High Executioner, was performed

by Grossmith, but though he had less to do than usual, he made a great deal of the part. His song on the

MISS L. BRAHAM AS YUM-YUM

finding a victim for his office was an immense success, and ingeniously adapted to current society topics:

As some day it may happen that a victim must be found
I've got a little list—I've got a little list
Of social offenders who might well be underground,

M

And who never would be missed—who never would be missed.

There's the pestilential nuisances who write for autographs—

MR. B. TEMPLE AS THE MIKADO

All people who have flabby hands and irritating laughs—

All children who are up in dates, and floor you with them flat—

All persons who in shaking hands shake hands with you like *that*—

And all third persons who on spoiling *tête-à-têtes* insist—

They'd none of 'em be missed—they'd none of 'em be missed.

The Mikado, pleasantly given by Temple, chatters with his officials over their impending execution and the manner of it.

Mik. Yes. *Something lingering, with boiling oil in it, I fancy.* Something of that sort. I think boiling oil occurs in it, but I'm not sure. I know it's something humorous, but lingering, with either boiling oil or melted lead. Come, come, don't fret—I'm not a bit angry.

Ko. (*in abject terror*). If your Majesty will accept our assurance, we had no idea——

Mik. Of course you hadn't. That's the pathetic part of it. Unfortunately the fool of an Act says, 'compassing the death of the heir apparent.' There's not a word about a mistake, or not knowing, or having no notion. There should be, of course, but there isn't. *That's the slovenly way in which these Acts are drawn.* However, cheer up, it'll be all right. I'll have it altered next session.

Ko. What's the good of that?

Mik. Now let's see—will after luncheon suit you? Can you wait till then?

Ko., Pitti, *and* Pooh. Oh yes—we can wait till then!

Mik. *Then we'll make it after luncheon.* I'm really very sorry for you all, but it's an unjust world, and virtue is triumphant only in theatrical performances.[1]

As the 'Mikado' is perhaps the *chef d'œuvre* of the author, and is best known and appreciated both at home and abroad, I may venture to quote the official judgment of a very competent critic and skilled musician, my friend Mr. Beatty-Kingston.

'The "Mikado" proved to be an extravaganza of the old Savoy type—a fabric in which familiar material has been

[1] Once passing through a small Dutch town I saw on a dead wall a tattered, fluttering poster, on which I read that 'Het *Mikado*, van Gilbert—Sullivan' was to be performed. In December 1893 the *Mikado* was revived at the Unter den Linden Theatre, Berlin, when to the composer's annoyance it was announced that a female performer, Frau von Palmay, would take the part of Nanki-Poo. The composer was much distressed at this travesty of his work, and made vigorous protest; but without avail. The lady duly appeared. *Utopia* was also to be performed in the same city, at the Friedrich-Wilhelm Stadtische Theatre.

cleverly worked up into a dainty Japanese pattern. Anachronisms, surprises, incongruities—unsparing exposure of human weaknesses and follies—things grave and even horrible invested with a ridiculous aspect—all the motives prompting our actions traced back to inexhaustible sources of selfishness and cowardice—a strange, uncanny frivolity indicated in each individual delineation of character, as though the author were bent upon subtly hinting to the audience that every one of his *dramatis personæ* is more or less intellectually deranged ; these are the leading characteristics exhibited by Mr. Gilbert's latest operatic libretto in common with its predecessors. Mr. Gilbert is a past-master in the craft of getting his puppets into and out of scrapes with an agreeable recklessness as to the ethics of their *modus operandi*. The executioner, commanded to do the duties of his office, which he has fraudulently suffered to fall into abeyance, instantly looks about him for some innocent victim, and bribes such an one with his own betrothed bride to perish in his stead. The cumulative official, a very nonpareil of infamy, expresses his pride in his ancestry by the basest venality. This view is really rendered imperative by the circumstance that their dearest personal interests are, throughout the plot, made dependent upon the infliction of a violent death upon one or other of them. Decapitation, disembowelment, immersion in boiling oil or molten lead are the eventualities upon which their attention (and that of the audience) is kept fixed with gruesome persistence. Mr. Gilbert has done his self-appointed work with surpassing ability and inimitable *verve*. The text of the "Mikado" sparkles with countless gems of wit—brilliants of the finest water—and its author's rhyming and rhythmic gifts have never been more splendidly displayed than in some of the verses assigned to Ko-Ko, Pooh-Bah, Yum-Yum, and the Mikado himself. As for the dialogue, it is positively so full of points and hits as to keep the wits of the audience constantly on the strain, scarcely ever affording to it an instant's repose or even respite from a rapid succession of smart and pungent incitements to mirth. In his case, supply has created demand; and it is he who has formed public taste in a particular direction, as it is only given to geniuses to do. Whether or not that direction be a salutary one is perhaps not very much to the purpose. He has unquestionably succeeded in imbuing society with his own quaint, scornful, inverted philosophy; and has thereby established a solid claim to rank amongst the foremost of those latter-day Englishmen who have exercised a distinct psychical influence upon their contemporaries.

'Sullivan is every whit as genuine a humorist as Gilbert, with this difference, that the *amari aliquid* never crops up in his compositions. They are always genial,

graceful, and, above all, beautiful; never more so than in
the score of the "Mikado." They twinkle with kindly,
sly fun; nothing in them ever grates harshly upon the
ear; they are exquisitely congruous to the sentiments or
situations which they profess to musically depict or reflect. What a graphic and fertile melodist is Sullivan!
What an accomplished orchestrator! How complete are
his knowledge and mastery of instrumental resources!
Of what other composer of our time can it with truth
be said that he is inexhaustible alike in invention
and contrivance? This is the ninth of his operas,
written in conjunction with Gilbert; and I, for my part,
should be greatly embarrassed to award the palm to any
one of them in particular, so excellent are they all. The
best proof, indeed, of the equality of their merits is the
fact that no two musicians are agreed as to which is
really the best of them. Beyond a doubt the "Mikado"
is as good as any of its forerunners. It contains half-a-
dozen numbers, each of which is sufficiently attractive to
ensure the opera's popularity; musical jewels of great
price, all aglow with the lustre of a pure and luminous
genius. Amongst these is a madrigal of extraordinary
beauty, written in the fine old scholarly English fashion
that comes to Sullivan as easily nowadays as it came of
yore to Wilbye and Battishill. "Hearts do not break," a
contralto song, which elicited a storm of applause from
as critical an audience as could well be assembled within

the walls of a London theatre, is Handelian in its breadth, and Schumannesque in its passionate force. The duet between Yum-Yum and Nanki-Poo, " Were I not to Ko-Ko plighted " (act i.), is simply charming. There is no prettier number in the opera than this ; but the great success of the evening—as far as reiterate and rapturous recalls were concerned, at least—was the trio and chorus, " Three little maids from school " (act i.), which the first-nighters insisted upon hearing three times, and would gladly have listened to a fourth, had not their request been steadfastly declined. Nothing fresher, gayer, or more captivating has ever bid for public favour than this delightful composition.'

This is a fair and judicious estimate, more than justified by the later popularity of the piece. It is extraordinary that a work which has been cordially appreciated in foreign countries should have never had a trial in France—an exclusion which, however, has extended to almost every English work of reputation. It is hardly invidious to impute this to an unworthy feeling of jealousy, or at least dislike. On some points our ' lively neighbours ' show themselves to be ' the spoiled child ' of Europe.

An entirely original supernatural opera, in two acts, first produced at the Savoy Theatre, by Mr. R. D'Oyly Carte, on Saturday, January 22, 1887.

RUDDIGORE

Dramatis Personæ

MORTALS

ROBIN OAKAPPLE (a Young Farmer) . .	MR. GEORGE GROSSMITH
RICHARD DAUNTLESS (his Foster-brother—a Man-o'-war's-man)	MR. DURWARD LELY
SIR DESPARD MURGATROYD (of Ruddigore—a Wicked Baronet)	MR. RUTLAND BARRINGTON
OLD ADAM GOODHEART (Robin's Faithful Servant)	MR. RUDOLPH LEWIS
ROSE MAYBUD (a Village Maiden) . .	MISS LEONORA BRAHAM
MAD MARGARET	MISS JESSIE BOND
DAME HANNAH (Rose's Aunt) . .	MISS ROSINA BRANDRAM
ZORAH } (Professional Bridesmaids) .	MISS JOSEPHINE FINDLAY
RUTH }	MISS LINDSAY

GHOSTS

SIR RUPERT MURGATROYD (the First Baronet) . .	MR. PRICE
SIR JASPER MURGATROYD (the Third Baronet) . .	MR. CHARLES
SIR LIONEL MURGATROYD (the Sixth Baronet) .	MR. TREVOR
SIR CONRAD MURGATROYD (the Twelfth Baronet) . .	MR. BURBANK
SIR DESMOND MURGATROYD (the Sixteenth Baronet) .	MR. TUER
SIR GILBERT MURGATROYD (the Eighteenth Baronet) .	MR. WILBRAHAM
SIR MERVYN MURGATROYD (the Twentieth Baronet) .	MR. COX

AND

SIR RODERIC MURGATROYD (the Twenty-first Baronet)	MR. RICHARD TEMPLE

Chorus of Officers, Ancestors, and Professional Bridesmaids

ACT I.—The Fishing Village of Rederring, in Cornwall

ACT II.—Picture Gallery in Ruddigore Castle

TIME.—EARLY IN THE PRESENT CENTURY

After a nearly two years' successful run, during which time the 'Mikado' was chanted everywhere and danced to in every ballroom, it became time to provide it with a successor. This was a difficulty, for, as it has often been shown, the successful man is really his own, and his chief dangerous competitor. The new opera was the only one of the series that was destined to be ill-appreciated by the public; yet it seemed to me had extraordinary merit both in story and music. This was 'Ruddigore,'[1] a very original and striking thing, affecting us with somewhat of the same emotions as did 'Les Cloches de Corneville.' A scene or two was suggested by an old piece of the author's written for the German Reeds, and called 'Ages Ago.' There was a tone of 'Monk' Lewis. The combination of the ghostly element with ordinary life was happily contrived. But it is the picturesque figures and quaint costumes that linger in the memory. These were really unfamiliar and treated in an original way. The story was in harmony, and inspired the composer with some impressive, solid music. The figure of Sir Rupert Murgatroyd, with his cap and

---

[1] With an odd crotchetiness, often exhibited by the public, much unmeaning objection was taken to the title. This, owing to a printer's mistake, had been announced as *Ruddygore*. A friend wrote gravely to remonstrate against such a title as 'Bloodygore.' 'When the press shuddered with convulsive horror (as it did) at the detestable title, I endeavoured to induce my *collaborateur* to consent to the title being changed to "Kensington Gore—or Robin and Richard were two pretty men," as being more idyllic—but Sullivan wouldn't consent.'—GILBERT.

tassel and long braided frock, the flowing cloak of the
period, was all striking enough. The picture gallery at
Ruddigore Castle, with the long perspective of family
full-length portraits stretching away, was most effective

DAME HANNAH, MISS BRANDRAM   ROSE, MISS BRAHAM

and poetical. These portraits were strictly and accu-
rately copied from the members of the chorus they
represented ; and it was an ingenious and striking effect
when the living figures, having taken the places of the
counterfeit presentments, descended solemnly from their

frames. The music of this scene was really appropriate, and a picturesque effect was produced by the assemblage of all the different uniforms of the English army, new and old ; these strange, old-fashioned equipments, defiling before us, left a curious ghostly feeling. The following conceit, though a little ' wire-drawn,' is worked out with much elaborate ingenuity :

Rob. Really I don't know what you'd have. I've only been a bad baronet a week, and I've committed a crime punctually every day. . . . (*Melodramatically*). On Wednesday I forged a will.

Sir Rod. Whose will ?

Rob. My own.

Sir Rod. My good sir, you can't forge you own will !

Rob. Can't I though ! I like that ! I *did* ! Besides, if a man can't forge his own will, whose will can he forge ?

1st Ghost. There's something in that.

2nd Ghost. Yes, it seems reasonable.

3rd Ghost. At first sight it does.

4th Ghost. Fallacy somewhere, I fancy !

Rob. A man can do what he likes with his own ?

Sir Rod. I suppose he can.

Rob. Well, then, he can forge his own will, stoopid ! On Thursday I shot a fox.

1st Ghost. Hear, hear !

Sir Rod. That's better (*addressing ghosts*). Pass the fox, I think ? (*They assent.*) Yes, pass the fox. Friday ?

Rob. On Friday I forged a cheque.

Sir Rod. Whose cheque ?

Rob. Old Adam's.

Sir Rod. But Old Adam hasn't a banker.

Rob. I didn't say I forged his banker—I said I forged his cheque. On Saturday I disinherited my only son.

Sir Rod. But you haven't got a son.

Rob. No—not yet. I disinherited him in advance, to save time. You see, by this arrangement he'll be born ready disinherited.

I have always thought the Salvationist duet between Sir Despard and Mad Margaret one of the most

MR. LELY, MISS BRAHAM, AND MR. GROSSMITH

diverting and really original of grotesque conceptions. Writer, composer, and singers furnished each an incomparable fund of quaintness. The music was as strange as the words, and the performers, again, were quite as good as words and music.

Des. I once was a very abandoned person—
Mar. Making the most of evil chances.
Des. Nobody could conceive a worse 'un—

MAR. Even in all the old romances.

DES. I blush for my wild extravagances,
   But be so kind
   To bear in mind,

MAR. We were the victims of circumstances!   (*Dance.*)
   That is one of our blameless dances.

MAR. I was an exceedingly odd young lady—

DES. Suffering much from spleen and vapours.

MAR. Clergymen thought my conduct shady—

DES. She didn't spend much upon linendrapers.

MAR. It certainly entertained the gapers.
   My ways were strange
   Beyond all range—

DES. And paragraphs got into all the papers.   (*Dance.*)
   We only cut respectable capers.

DES. I've given up all my wild proceedings.

MAR. My taste for a wandering life is waning.

DES. Now I'm a dab at penny readings.

MAR. They are not remarkably entertaining.

DES. A moderate livelihood we're gaining.

MAR.   In fact, we rule
   A National School.

DES. The duties are dull, but I'm not complaining.
          (*Dance.*)
  This sort of thing takes a deal of training!

Who will forget the extraordinary oddity and abruptness of the break for the dance, followed by the strange exclamation, as if in reverie:

  This sort of thing takes a deal of training?

We could have heard that ditty—after its second

encore—repeated again and again. We should wish to hear it now, but there is little likelihood of its being revived.

Sir Roderic's talk with the picture-ghosts exhibits our author's ingenious conceits and playings with words at their best.

MISS BOND   MISS BRANDRAM   MR. BARRINGTON   MR. BARRINGTON

The absurdity or 'banality' of the operatic chorus offering their unmeaning greetings is thus happily satirised:

BRIDESMAIDS

Hail the bridegroom—hail the bride!
Let the nuptial knot be tied:

In fair phrases
Hymn their praises,
Hail the bridegroom—hail the bride !

    Welcome, gentry,
    For your entry
Sets our tender hearts a-beating.
    Men of station,
    Admiration
Prompts this unaffected greeting.
       Hearty greeting offer we !

The odd conceits of the following meditation often recur :

    Cheerily carols the lark
      Over the cot.
    Merrily whistles the clerk
      Scratching a blot.
      But the lark
      And the clerk,
      I remark,
    Comfort me not !

    Over the ripening peach
      Buzzes the bee.
    Splash on the billowy beach
      Tumbles the sea.
      But the peach
      And the beach
      They are each
    Nothing to me !

Again :

    Maidens, greet her,
    Kindly treat her,
You may all be brides some day.

And this warning—to a droll rhyme:

> O innocents, listen in time,
> Avoid an existence of crime
> *Or you'll be as ugly as I'm.*

And:

> Agricultural employment
> Is to me a keen enjoyment.

And there are some other quaint strokes, ingenious, too, in their rhyme and reason:

> I abandon propriety,
> Visit the haunts of Bohemian society,
> Waxworks and other resorts of impiety,
> Placed by the moralist under a ban. . . .

> O wretched the debtor who's signing a deed,
> And wretched the letter that no one can read;
> But very much better, their lot it must be
> Than that of the person I'm making this verse on,
> Whose head there's a curse on—alluding to me. . . .

> Mad, I?
> Yes, very.
> But why!
> Mystery! . . .

> He's in easy circumstances;
> Young and lusty,
> True and trusty.

There are other instances of the special humour to which our author is so partial:

N

Han. Nay, dear one, where true love is, there is little need of prim formality.

Rose. Hush, dear aunt, for thy words pain me sorely. Hung in a plated dish-cover to the knocker of the workhouse door, with nought that I could call mine own save a change of baby-linen and a book of etiquette, little wonder if I have always regarded that work as a voice from a parent's tomb.

THE FISHING VILLAGE OF REDERRING

This hallowed volume (*producing a book of etiquette*), composed, if I may believe the title-page, by no less an authority than the wife of a Lord Mayor, has been, through life, my guide and monitor. By its solemn precepts I have learnt to test the moral worth of all who approach me. The man who bites his bread, or eats peas with a knife, I look upon as a lost creature, and he who has not acquired the proper way of entering and leaving a room is the object of my pitying horror. There are those in this village who bite their nails, dear aunt, and nearly all are wont to use their pocket-combs in public places. In truth, I could pursue this painful theme much further, but behold, I have said enough.

Now this, as a form of burlesque, seems a little imperfect. The utterer of these quips was conscious of the absurdity, yet appears to be superior to it.[1]

So with that odd notion in ' Ruddigore ' of using a word which shall recall Mad Margaret to sobriety—' some word that teems with hidden meaning, like "Basingstoke," might recall me to my saner self.' Despard says :

But soft, someone comes. Margaret, pray recollect yourself. *Basingstoke, I beg*. Margaret, if you don't Basingstoke at once, I shall be seriously angry.

Margaret (*recovering herself*). Basingstoke it is.

Des. Then make it so.

MR. D. LELY
AS RICHARD DAUNTLESS

This is whimsical enough in the treatment, but the conceit itself is a trifling one.

---

[1] Our author, however, urges that ' Rose's dealing with the book of etiquette should not be self-conscious ; she is perfectly in earnest, and should display no sense of any incongruity.' Still, the theme is so developed that this unconsciousness can only be secured by the assumption of some mental deficiency.

I must confess, too, that the point of the following
is not intelligible—to me, at least :

> Ron. Soho! pretty one—in my power at last, eh? Know
> ye not that I have those within my call who, at my lightest
> bidding, would immure ye in an uncomfortable dungeon?
> (*Calling.*) What ho! within there!
>
> Rich. Hold—we are prepared for this (*producing a Union
> Jack*). Here is a flag that none dare defy (*all kneel*), and
> while this glorious rag floats over Rose Maybud's head, the
> man does not live who would dare to lay unlicensed hand
> upon her!
>
> Ron. Foiled—and by a Union Jack! But a time will
> come, and then——

It was in ' Ruddigore,' too, that a burlesque allusion
produced a storm of indignation in our neighbours across
the Channel. This was really intended to ridicule the
Chauvinist boastings of the old days, but the French took
it literally, and insisted that it was an actual affront.[1]

After ' Ruddigore ' had run its rather short course it
became known that the Savoy troupe was to ' shed ' yet
another of its leading members. The loss of Grossmith
was impending; but it was now learned that Barrington,
the inimitable Pooh-Bah, had seceded. Once the two props
of the house had gone, the same spirit was to affect the
principals themselves. Durward Lely, that finished tenor,
was soon to depart; his successor, Courtice Pounds, was

[1] Some thirty French officers actually engaged to call the author to
account.

to follow. Jessie Bond, after a long service, was to go also. This seems to be of the essence of such associations.

After some years of this agreeable service, and crowded, applauding houses every night, the generic tenor begins to think, almost as a matter of course, that he was made for better things, or at least for a better salary. This he usually demands, and on demur resigns his pleasant, easy post. Friends assure him that with his reputation he is 'worth double,' and will get double. Too late he finds out that nothing can make up for the steady permanence of his former situation : he discovers to his surprise that most of his reputation is owing to the very theatre itself, and to the works in which he has figured. Too late he finds the precariousness and uncertainty of all things outside that favoured temple, where, in the words of the facetious song, ' He never will be missed—he never will be missed.' Return is impossible, as his place is filled without difficulty.

There was one exception, however—that of Barrington, who at this time was seized with a hunger for management. A friendly financier offered to back his enterprise, and with the genial goodwill of his late associates, and universal good wishes, the pleasant Corcoran, Dr. Daly, &c., embarked on management at the St. James's Theatre. Gilbert furnished him with a comedy, ' Brantinghame Hall,' and also with a new actress, Julia

Neilson, of whom he had a high opinion, which on this occasion I fancied she scarcely justified. It must be said that his judgment in these matters is far-seeing and goes deep, and the lady, as we know, has turned out a very striking and sympathetic performer. 'Brantinghame Hall,' however, was not acceptable, though the author had great faith in the piece; and it must be confessed that it somewhat lacked coherence.[1]   Barrington made some other experiments, which were rather disastrous, and at last was glad to resign the ill-fated venture and return to his old house, where he was at home, and where he was received with open arms by management and audience. With these old friends he has wisely continued ever since.

[1] 'Miss Neilson,' wrote the author to me on the day after the performance, 'was absolutely paralysed with nervousness last night. In a few days she will do herself justice. It was a tremendous ordeal for a young girl who has only walked a stage eight times in her life, and who never played an original part before.' Our author then explained his purpose in the piece. 'The villain might easily and effectively have been baffled by the arrival of the parson, as you suggest; but I didn't want the villain to be an "out-and-outer," but rather a man led to the commission of unworthy deeds through overmastering passion—rather a good fellow than otherwise; at all events, a man with good and generous impulses, which occasionally assert themselves. This is hinted at when he arrives at Brantinghame prepared to deal loyally with Lord Saxondham.'

Produced at the Savoy Theatre, under the management of Mr. R. D'Oyly Carte, on Wednesday, October 3, 1888.

THE YEOMEN OF THE GUARD

OR

THE MERRYMAN AND HIS MAID

Dramatis Personæ

SIR RICHARD CHOLMONDELEY (*Lieutenant of the Tower*)	MR. W. BROWNLOW
COLONEL FAIRFAX (*under sentence of death*) .	MR. COURTICE POUNDS
SERGEANT MERYLL (*of the Yeomen of the Guard*)	MR. RICHARD TEMPLE
LEONARD MERYLL (*his Son*)	MR. W. R. SHIRLEY
JACK POINT (*a Strolling Jester*) . . .	MR. GEORGE GROSSMITH
WILFRED SHADBOLT (*Head Gaoler and Assistant Tormentor*) . . .	MR. W. H. DENNY
THE HEADSMAN . . .	MR. RICHARDS
FIRST YEOMAN . . .	MR. WILBRAHAM
SECOND ,, . . .	MR. METCALF
THIRD ,, . .	MR. MERTON
FOURTH ,, . . .	MR. RUDOLF LEWIS
FIRST CITIZEN . . .	MR. REDMOND
SECOND ,, ...	MR. BOYD
ELSIE MAYNARD (*a Strolling Singer*) .	MISS GERALDINE ULMAR
PHŒBE MERYLL (*Sergeant Meryll's Daughter*) .	MISS JESSIE BOND
DAME CARRUTHERS (*Housekeeper to the Tower*) .	MISS ROSINA BRANDRAM
KATE (*her Niece*)	MISS ROSE HERVEY

Chorus of Yeomen of the Guard, Gentlemen, Citizens, &c.

SCENE.—Tower Green

DATE.—SIXTEENTH CENTURY

In this piece, the 'Yeomen of the Guard,' our author adopted quite a new method; there was a pleasing, interesting episode, treated with sincerity and

seriously, though set off with a fringe, as it were, of
lively conceits. The picturesque locality of the Tower
all but inspired the story. There was a prisoner of

Phœbe Meryll — Miss Jessie Bond

state, one Colonel Fairfax, sentenced to be executed;
there was the gaoler and his daughter, the lieutenant,
a 'strolling jester,' and, of course, ready to hand a
picturesque chorus, the 'Beefeaters.' The tale is

simple and unassuming, and something in the vein of
G. P. R. James or Ainsworth.   The prisoner, taking the

'Sergeant Meryll' — Mr Richard Temple

place of the sergeant's son, is enrolled in the guard as a
recruit; the gaoler is in love with Phœbe and is 'flouted'

by her; there is a prison marriage, too, before the execution, and at the end all are made happy. The composer, too, was fortunate in being furnished with such a story to set. It supplied him with some stately, well-coloured ideas; he evidently was inspired by the picturesque

COLONEL FAIRFAX.

locale; his strains reflect the influence of the grim old precinct:

> Ye towers of Julius! London's lasting shame!
> By many a foul and midnight murder fed.

At the same time it was felt that here was a departure from the stricter traditions of the Savoy.

Grossmith was allotted a curious part, a sort of

mediæval jester called Jack Point. It was somewhat
artificial in its cast, but he made a very piquant
character of it. To him was allotted the beautiful air,
' I have a song to sing O ! ' with drone accompaniment,
one of the most charming of
Sullivan's efforts. It made
a deep impression, and chimes
in our ears at this very moment.

It is thus that composers
so often really make the public
a present of something that
they can take home with them
and put by, and which can be
used and renewed again and
again to recreate themselves
with on occasion.

The fooling of this fool is
a little archaic, though no
doubt it was intended as a
satire on the salaried quips of these gentry. The lieutenant asks him :

And how came you to leave your last employ ?

Point. Why, sir, it was in this wise. My lord was the
Archbishop of Canterbury, and it was considered that one of
my jokes was unsuited to his Grace's family circle. In truth
I ventured to ask a poor riddle, sir—Wherein lay the difference between his Grace and poor Jack Point ? His

Grace was pleased to give it up, sir. And thereupon I told
him that whereas his Grace was paid 10,000*l.* a year for
being good, poor Jack Point was good—for nothing. 'Twas
but a harmless jest, but it offended his Grace, who whipped me
and set me in the stocks for a scurril rogue, and so we parted.
I had as lief not take post again with the dignified clergy.

    .   .   .   .

    LIEUT. Can you give me an example? Say that I had sat
me down hurriedly on something sharp?

WILFRED SHADBOLT.

    POINT. Sir, I should say that you had sat down on the
spur of the moment.

    LIEUT. Humph. I don't think much of that. Is that
the best you can do?

    POINT. It has always been much admired, sir, but we will
try again.

    LIEUT. Well then, I am at dinner, and the joint of meat
is but half cooked.

    POINT. Why then, sir, I should say—that what is *under*-
done cannot be helped.

LIEUT. I see. I think that manner of thing would be somewhat irritating.

THE SOCIETY CLOWN

POINT. At first, sir, perhaps; but use is everything, and you would come in time to like it.

LIEUT. We will suppose that I caught you kissing the kitchen wench under my very nose.

POINT. Under *her* very nose, good sir—not under yours! *That* is where *I* would kiss her. Do you take me? Oh, sir, a pretty wit—a pretty, pretty wit!

MISS JESSIE BOND AND MR. W. H. DENNY AS PHŒBE MERYLL AND
WILFRED SHADBOLT

LIEUT. The maiden comes. Follow me, friend, and we will discuss this matter at length in my library.

He afterwards sings with pleasant humour of the hard lot of the 'private buffoon' who is checked by the dullards at every turn.

Among the performers was found a new recruit, who
had long served under the Bancrofts at the old Totten-
ham Court Road Theatre, and who has the art of im-

THE YEOMEN
OF THE
SAVOY.

parting to even minor characters a sort of individuality.
This was Denny. He has a dry, self-contained, reserved
humour, which was shown effectually in the part of the
Tower gaoler. He has since taken his place as one

of the props of the house. He is, however, somewhat *borné* in his gifts, and, though a sound and conscientious performer, has but a limited range.

Performed at the Savoy Theatre, under the management of Mr. R. D'Oyly Carte, on Saturday, December 7, 1889, an entirely original comic opera, in two acts.

THE GONDOLIERS
OR
THE KING OF BARATARIA

Dramatis Personæ

THE DUKE OF PLAZA-TORO (*a Grandee of Spain*)	MR. FRANK WYATT
LUIZ (*his Attendant*)	MR. BROWNLOW
DON ALHAMBRA DEL BOLERO (*the Grand Inquisitor*)	MR. DENNY
MARCO PALMIERI	MR. COURTICE POUNDS
GIUSEPPE PALMIERI	MR. RUTLAND BARRINGTON
ANTONIO	MR. METCALF
FRANCESCO (*Venetian Gondoliers*)	MR. ROSE
GIORGIO	MR. DE PLEDGE
ANNIBALE	MR. WILBRAHAM
OTTAVIO	MR. C. GILBERT
THE DUCHESS OF PLAZA-TORO . .	MISS ROSINA BRANDRAM
CASILDA (*her Daughter*) . . .	MISS DECIMA MOORE
GIANETTA	MISS GERALDINE ULMAR
TESSA	MISS JESSIE BOND
FIAMETTA (*Contadine*) . . .	MISS LAWRENCE
VITTORIA	MISS COLE
GIULIA	MISS PHYLLIS
INEZ (*the King's Foster-mother*) . .	MISS BERNARD

Chorus of Gondoliers and Contadine, Men-at-arms, Heralds, and Pages

ACT I.—The Piazetta, Venice
ACT II.—Pavilion in the Palace of Barataria

The 'Gondoliers,' for sparkle, show, brilliant dresses, and lively music, was one of the most attractive of the series. The tunes were taking—the composer sought to impart a kind of local colour—the measures were half Italian or Spanish, with the usual fandangoes, boleros, &c. For a practised musician this is easy enough, and is, indeed, a sort of common form. The story was ingeniously compounded, though the idea is suggested that it was put together a little capriciously. When the public came to welcome the new opera it knew that one of its oldest favourites would be no longer there to entertain them. George Grossmith, the enjoyable 'Gee-Gee,' had departed. This was a serious loss. A Savoy opera without this grotesque, mercurial, central figure was almost inconceivable. There was no substitute to be found. He stood out quite brilliantly from the background. To this hour it may be doubted if the Savoy opera is the same thing that it was in those days.

He was led to take this step by the reflection that for some years he had been losing money by his engagement, possibly to the amount of one or two hundred a week. His salary of 40*l.* or 50*l.* was handsome, and about as much as the manager of a costly theatre could afford; 2,000*l.* a year is no bad allowance. But he had long felt that there was a great field open to his talents in the entertainment direction. He had already made his mark in this way, and after his performance

o

at the Savoy used to repair to fashionable entertainments, where he gave his songs and recitations. Golden profits opened before him; and with such profit all but a certainty, it would have been folly to resist, and so he took this important step. The success, as he has assured me, has exceeded his most sanguine expectations.[1]

This shows how utopian—in these days at least—is the notion of a good all-round company whose chief members are of equal merit. Philosophers tell us that such is the ideal system to be found at the Théâtre Français. But it is no sooner constituted than it must dissolve, for the very reason that influenced Grossmith—viz. every member of conspicuous merit is playing at a loss, and feels that he could make three or four times as much. For this compelling reason the Français is gradually snedding its leading members; witness Sarah Bernhardt, Coquelin, and others.

The Savoy corps has during fourteen or fifteen years seen other changes. Save, perhaps, Barrington and Miss Brandram, nearly all the original prominent members have gone—Grossmith, Durward Lely, George Power,

---

[1] Still, as if to prove that neither pelf nor the comparative gain of the platform will make up for the glittering attraction of the scene, there have lately been rumours of his return to the domain of his old triumphs. It has been stated in various journals that in case of a revival of the *Mikado* or the *Yeomen of the Guard*—indistinctly shadowed forth—our friend would resume his old character.

Jessie Bond, the Temples, and many more. The present members now carry on the traditions, but do not originate. Denny, it would appear, is held out as a sort of successor to Grossmith, but is unequal, and has not the magic touch.

The 'Gondoliers' introduced quite an array of new talent, with a large number of characters. The management seemed to have thought that 'fresh blood' was wanting for the enterprise, and the recent loss of Grossmith warned them that they could not rely on the permanent stay of old favourites. We found on this occasion several new performers who had served in the ranks of the Savoy

A LEADING LADY

country corps. We had the versatile Frank Wyatt, who could not only sing but 'danced like an angel';

rather, like Mr. Fezziwig in the story, he could 'cut so deftly that he seemed to wink with his legs.' There was also another agreeable, well-taught singer, Brownlow— more baritone than tenor. Among the ladies there was a new candidate for Savoy favour—Miss Decima Moore, a piquant actress with a sweet and flexible voice, who was cordially welcomed.[1] Miss Geraldine Ulmar was the titular prima donna.

In this piece the author has very happily touched off the conventional operatic notion of gondoliers, and those scraps of accepted Italian which the tourist brings back with him :

> Giu. *and* Mar. (*their arms full of flowers.*)   O ciel !
> Girls. Buon' giorno, cavalieri !
> Giu. *and* Mar. (*deprecatingly*). Siamo gondolieri.
>   (*to* Fia. *and* Vit). Signorina, io t' amo !
> Girls. (*deprecatingly*). Contadine siamo.
> Giu. *and* Mar. Signorine !
> Girls (*deprecatingly*). Contadine !
>   (*curtseying to* Giu. *and* Mar.) Cavalieri.
> Giu. *and* Mar. (*deprecatingly*). Gondolieri !
>   Poveri gondolieri !
> Chorus. Buon' giorno, signorine, &c.

> Duet—Marco *and* Giuseppe
>   We're called *gondolieri*,
>   But that's a vagary,
>   It's quite honorary
>   The trade that we ply.

<hr>

[1] Miss Moore came from the Brixton Conservatoire, where she was a promising singer, and, like Miss McPherson, made her first appearance on

> For gallantry noted
> Since we were short-coated
> To ladies devoted,
>> My brother and I.

The conventional dance, too, of the sprightly children of the South is capitally symbolised in these lines, which the composer set to music artfully compounded of the usual hackneyed forms :

> We will dance a cachucha, fandango, bolero,
> Old Xeres we'll drink—Manzanilla, Montero—
> For wine, when it runs in abundance, enhances
> The reckless delight of that wildest of dances!
>> To the pretty pitter-pitter-patter,
>> And the clitter-clitter-clitter-clatter—
>>> Clitter—clitter—clatter,
>>> Pitter—pitter—patter—
> We will dance a cachucha, fandango, bolero.

Sometimes our author falls into a mood of moralising, and these lines have a pleasant philosophy, carried off by a faint *soupçon* of banter :

> Try we lifelong, we can never
>> Straighten out life's tangled skein,
> Why should we, in vain endeavour,
>> Guess and guess and guess again ?
>>> Life's a pudding full of plums,
>>> Care's a canker that benumbs.

any stage on this occasion. She had been engaged to figure in Mr. Burnand's adaptation, *Miss Decima*, which had been a bizarre combination.

Wherefore waste our elocution
On impossible solution ?
Life's a pleasant institution,
    Let us take it as it comes !

This was set in the form of one of those taking, well-harmonised concerted quintettes which are found scattered

MISS MOORE   MR. POUNDS   MR. F. WYATT   MISS BRANDRAM

through these operas, often unaccompanied. They were always listened to with an almost breathless attention, and at the close a burst of tumultuous applause enforced their repetition.

One of the utopian schemes of the grotesque duke was the establishing of a general equality; thus anticipating a little what was to be the subject of a regular opera:

> The earl, the marquis, and the dook,
> The groom, the butler, and the cook,
> The aristocrat who banks with Coutts,
> The aristocrat who cleans the boots,
> The noble lord who rules the State,
> The noble lord who scrubs the grate,
> The Lord High Bishop orthodox,
> The Lord High Vagabond in the stocks—
> > Sing high, sing low,
> > Wherever they go,
> > They all shall equal be!

And in a most amusing duet the duke and duchess play upon the theme with wonderful variety:

DUCH. When Virtue would quash her,
  I take and whitewash her,
   And launch her in first-rate society—
DUKE.   First-rate society!
DUCH. I recommend acres
  Of clumsy dressmakers—
   Their fit and their finishing touches—
DUKE.   Their finishing touches.
DUCH. A sum in addition
  They pay for permission
   To say that they make for the duchess—
DUKE.   They make for the duchess!

DUCH. At middle-class party
    I play at *écarté*—
        And I'm by no means a beginner—
DUKE (*significantly*). She's not a beginner.
DUCH. To one of my station
    The remuneration—
        Five guineas a night and my dinner—
DUKE.   And wine with her dinner.
DUCH. I write letters blatant
    On medicines patent—
        And use any other you mustn't—
DUKE.   Believe me, you mustn't—
DUCH. And vow my complexion
    Derives its perfection
        From somebody's soap—which it doesn't—
DUKE (*significantly*). It certainly doesn't!

Denny's song had one of those quaintly original refrains of which Gilbert has the secret:

I stole the prince, and I brought him here,
    And left him, gaily prattling,
With a highly respectable gondolier,
Who promised the royal babe to rear,
And teach him the trade of a timoneer
    With his own beloved bratling.
        Both of the babes were strong and stout,
            And, considering all things, clever.
        Of that there is no manner of doubt—
            No probable, possible shadow of doubt—
        No possible doubt whatever.

In the 'Gondoliers' there is a trite familiar process, treated in a humorous way. Giuseppe and Marco select

their 'girls' by the aid of 'Blindman's Buff,' to this
variation of the nursery lines :

> My papa he keeps three horses,
> Black, and white, and dapple grey, sir ;
> Turn three times, then take your courses,
> Catch whichever girl you may, sir !

Then follow these quaint rhymes :

GIANETTA

Thank you, gallant *gondolieri* :
         In a set and formal measure
It is scarcely necessary
         To express our pride and pleasure.
         Each of us to prove a treasure,
Conjugal and monetary,
         Gladly will devote our leisure,
Gay and gallant *gondolieri.*
         La, la, la, la, la ! &c.

TESSA

Gay and gallant *gondolieri,*
         Take us both and hold us tightly,
You have luck extraordinary ;
         We might both have been unsightly !
         If we judge your conduct rightly,
'Twas a choice involuntary ;
         Still, we thank you most politely,
Gay and gallant *gondolieri* !
         La, la, la, la, la ! &c.

The two kings declare that 'it is a very pleasant
existence,' everybody being so kind and considerate.

'You don't find them wanting to do this, or wanting to do that, or saying, "It's my turn now."' The notion of the duke making himself into a company, as the 'Duke of Plaza-Toro, Limited,' is a pleasant fancy. His speech to his sons-in-law is droll throughout:

DUKE. I am now about to address myself to the gentleman whom my daughter married; the other may allow his

THE DUKE

attention to wander if he likes, for what I am about to say does not concern him. Sir, you will find in this young lady a combination of excellences which you would search for in vain in any young lady who had not the good fortune to be my daughter. There is some little doubt as to which of you is the gentleman I am addressing, and which is the gentleman who is allowing his attention to wander; but when that

doubt is solved, I shall say (still addressing the attentive
gentleman), 'Take her, and may she make you happier than
her mother has made me.'

With the 'Gondoliers' returned to the Savoy fold
that prime, indeed all but necessary favourite, Rutland
Barrington.   His peculiar style—so free and unctuous,
yet judiciously reserved—has done much for the Savoy
opera; indeed it might probably be said that without
such interpreters as he and Grossmith the great success
would probably not have been attained.   His personality
is so marked that, though his methods are nearly always
the same, there is never left the impression of monotony
or sameness.   We listen with all the pleasure of novelty
to his efforts, and rarely fail to be recreated.   Here
is the 'note' of an artist.   His unfortunate venture at
the St. James's Theatre had not damped his spirit; and
his friends and admirers were unfeignedly glad to see him
back in his old haunts.

In this opera—the last presented of the series—it
was curious to note how largely the scale of treatment
had developed compared with the early and modest
pretensions of the 'Trial by Jury' and the 'Sorcerer.'
Then the whole burden was really on the shoulders
of a quartette or quintette, supported by an occasional
chorus, who recited their pleasant 'lilting' tunes and
ballads in an articulate fashion that brought out the
sense of every line.   But now, after nearly a score of

years, what a change! Here we had almost a grand
opera, with close on fifteen prominent, well-marked
characters, with an array of choristers, rich accompaniments, recitations and finales, all worked up according to
the approved canons. The composer's methods, too, have
enlarged with the canvas on which he worked. His
accompaniments are elaborate and flowing, and he has
clearly aimed at general musical treatment of the story
itself. It may be thought, indeed, that the Savoy opera
has now all but outgrown its habitation, and will hardly
admit of further expansion.

While the 'Gondoliers' was pursuing its prosperous
course and supplying enjoyment for thousands all over the
kingdom, its admirers were seriously disturbed at learning
that a little rift had appeared in the lute, and that
owing to a sudden estrangement the pleasant partnership had come to an end. At this news there was something like consternation. It unfortunately proved to be
true. A difference had arisen between the manager and
one of the partners, into which the other was presently
drawn. The discussion became so acute that a complete
breach followed ; and it was understood that the agreeable, mirth-giving alliance which for so many years had
increased the public stock of harmless pleasure was dissolved. For a time it was hoped that a reconciliation
would be effected, but the matter was too serious to be
compromised. As month after month went by without

signs of the breach being healed, audiences had to accept as best they could so unfortunate a state of things. We need not here discuss the causes of the quarrel, concerning which many rumours were afloat; but the *fons et origo* must have been serious, as the sacrifice involved was enormous, and to some extent irreparable. A great venture of this sort may not be interrupted or dislocated without permanent damage. It suggests the case of some too hasty resignation of office, the effects of which cannot be undone.

The partnership being thus dissolved, each of the partners sought out new assistants with whom to seek afresh the favour of the public. The intimate and even indissoluble character of the connection between the writer and the composer was shown in a very striking way during the period of the misunderstanding which separated them for a time. Each chose another coadjutor, and with the same result. Gilbert wrote one of his most amusing pieces, the 'Mountebanks,' which was duly set to music by Cellier, while Sullivan was supplied by Mr. Grundy with a play called 'Haddon Hall.' Of course a certain amount of success attended these productions, owing to the traditional popularity of the authors and the handsome style in which they were brought forward, but it was felt that the result was rather a specimen of the regular conventional opera—a libretto set to music

—than the favourite Savoy partnership, in which the share of each was equally prominent. 'Haddon Hall' had rather an old-fashioned Harrison Ainsworth tone. There were Cavaliers and Roundheads, concealments and pursuits, pert waiting-maids, and the rest. Denny was an impossible Scot, who danced the dances of his country, and furnished the composer with contrapuntal opportunities based on Caledonian modes, which he worked with his usual skill. It was curious that with each of these productions there were to be associated some exceptional incidents—one of a rather pathetic kind.

Though there was an attempt to reproduce the old Savoy patterns, there was a marked contrast between the new lyrics and those Savoy audiences had grown accustomed to ; witness—

Now isn't that beautiful, isn't that nice ?
 When I tell you the article's German,
You'll know it could only be sold at the price
 Through a grand international firman.
A still greater bargain ! an article French :
 When I say it's of French manufacture,
I mean that, if worn by a beautiful wench,
 A heart it is certain to fracture.
But here is the price—only tuppence—pure gold :
 When I mention the article's Yankee,
Well, nobody then will require to be told
 That there can't be the least hanky-panky !

MISS LUCILLE HILL AND MR.
COURTICE POUNDS AS DORO-
THY VERNON AND LORD JOHN
MANNERS

The composer must have felt strangely as he proceeded to set the last two lines. So with the Scotch song :

> My name it is McCrankie,
> I am lean, an' lang, an' lanky,
> I'm a Moody and a Sankey
> > Wound upo' a Scottish reel !
> Pedantic an' puncteelious,
> Severe an' superceelious,
> Preceese and atrabeelious—
> > But meanin' vera weel.

> I don't object tae weesky,
> But I say a' songs are risky,
> An' I think a' dances frisky,
> > An' I've put the fuitlichts oot !
> I am the maist dogmatical,
> Three-cornered, autocratical,
> Funereal, fanatical,
> > O' a' the cranks aboot !

One incident associated with 'Haddon Hall' was somewhat in the nature of an oddity, or dramatic 'curio.' Mr. Boulding, an industrious dramatist, had, it seems, written a piece on this subject, in good old legitimate blank verse, and with a sincerity and earnestness worthy of Sheridan Knowles himself. He complained, I believe, that he had been anticipated in the production. Mr. D'Oyly Carte very handsomely gave ear to these remonstrances, and with much liberality actually consented to place his theatre at the disposal

P

of the disappointed author for a morning performance. It oddly happened that the order of the scenes, &c., in the opera fitted very fairly with some of the scenes in the play. There was the grand, dazzling interior of the Hall, which was available, together with the handsome dresses. The whole passed off very well indeed, and was curious to follow. It seemed a sort of antique survival; and yet not unwelcome was the old declaimed blank verse, for so long unfamiliar. The audience was good-natured, and we may presume the author was content. The performance was certainly unique.

Another odd and rather surprising incident occurred during this interval. Gilbert had bethought himself of his old adaptation, ' A Wedding March,' which, it occurred to him, offered opportunities for being arranged as a comic opera. He set to work, fitted it out with verses for solos and chorus, leaving the main portion pretty much as it was. The extraordinary success in the old days of this very ' rollicking ' piece suggested to him that in this new shape it might be even more attractive. But who would do the music ? There was but a slender list of composers of this *genre*. Cellier, the author of the popular ' Dorothy '; Edward Solomon, a musician of much facility and variety, but who seems to have generally missed winning the public ear, were available, but were not thought of by our author. He had selected his coadjutor, and applied for aid—the reader will scarcely

guess to whom—to Grossmith. No one, I believe, was
more surprised than the pleasant 'Gee-Gee' himself at
the application; but he was at the same time not a little
flattered, and if at all distrustful of his own powers for
such a task, he was reassured by the author, who had
every confidence that he was suited to the task and that
the work was safe in his hands. In truth Grossmith
has a pleasant gift of composition, attested by his innumerable songs, which are spirited and dramatic.
Indeed, that delightful little parody of a light opera, the
'*Gay Markee*,' which exhibits all the conventional absur-
dities of such things, is not only comic to a degree,
but has some capital music.

I recall the night when, before a crowded house,
gathered to see this new exhibition of the favourite's
powers, he gaily stepped into the orchestra to conduct
the performance. There was a roguish smile on his
expressive face as he gravely went through the professional methods, tapping the desk for attention, &c. It
was really a wonderful thing under the conditions—of
course, with a strong flavour of imitation of his predecessors. The orchestration was a little weak, if not
thin, but on the whole it was a surprising *tour de force*,
and 'passed' very well. The worst was, the libretto
seemed a little superannuated, and, though once enjoying
brilliant success and drawing all the town, seemed now
to belong to a bygone era.

Gilbert was also busy preparing a new opera of the favourite pattern—the 'Mountebanks.' The music was to be furnished by Cellier, one of the two brothers, Alfred and François, who conducted the orchestra at the 'Savoy.' By this time the bright sparkling methods of the Savoy music had become familiar, and any deft, skilful musician could find cunning enough to copy or adapt the original tuneful devices. But apart from this almost unavoidable imitation of the popular style, the 'Mountebanks' proved to be a sound and musicianly piece, which was heard with a great deal of pleasure. It enjoyed much popularity and ran for a considerable time. It introduced for the first time a clever young singer, Aïda Jenoure, who created a quaint character founded on a Gilbertian conceit – the adaptation of 'the penny-in-the-slot' mechanism to the human figure.

The versatile Cellier—whose 'Dorothy' had some delightful 'numbers'—understood enough of Gilbert's methods to execute his task in a fairly satisfactory manner. But when he had nearly accomplished his task a mortal sickness with which he had been struggling became a serious interruption. Nothing could be more forbearing than the indulgence extended. Great interests were at stake; heavy engagements, pecuniary and other, were involved; but there was no pressure exerted beyond an appeal to do what he reasonably could. On his side the dying composer made heroic exertions to complete his task, compelled, as he was, every now and again to lay it aside. But he persevered, and had all but completed his work when the pen fell from his hand. There was something really fine in this story of self-sacrifice. Yet the music is sparkling and tuneful, and though somewhat lacking in inspiration, as might be expected, would never be supposed to have been engendered on a deathbed.[1]

---

[1] This unobtrusive man had done a great deal of work in his time, and contributed much to the recreation of the public. ' Alfred Cellier, although of French extraction, was born at Hackney on December 1, 1844, and, like Sir Arthur Sullivan, was originally a choir-boy at the Chapel Royal under the Rev. Thomas Helmore. After his voice failed he studied the organ, and as a lad of eighteen was appointed organist at All Saints', Blackheath. He then went to Belfast, but in 1868 he returned, as organist of St. Alban's, Holborn, to London, where, except as to four years as conductor at the Prince's Theatre, Manchester, and certain voyages to Australia and elsewhere, taken for purposes of health, he has since chiefly resided. For three years from 1877 he conducted the Gilbert and Sullivan operas at the Opera Comique, and in 1878–9 he was joint conductor with Sir Arthur Sullivan of the Promenade Concerts at Covent Garden. The earliest of his light operas, *Charity begins at Home*, was produced at the old Gallery of Illustration as far back as 1870, but four years later his *Sultan of Mocha*—originally produced at Manchester, and in 1876 given at the St. James's Theatre, London—brought him prominently into public notice. The *Tower of London* followed in 1875, and *Nell Gwynne* in 1876. The libretto of the last-named opera was afterwards reset by a French composer, and a good deal of the original music was, we believe, used up for *Dorothy*, which, produced in 1886 at the Gaiety, was afterwards transferred to the Prince of Wales's and the Lyric, and enjoyed a long and lucrative run. Among his other operas or operettas may be mentioned the *Spectre Knight* (written in collaboration with the late Mr. Albery for Mr. D'Oyly Carte), *Dora's Dream, After All*, the *Carp*, and *Doris*. He has likewise

*Produced at the Lyric Theatre, London, under the management
of Mr. Horace Sedger, on Monday, January 4, 1892.*

THE MOUNTEBANKS

Dramatis Personæ

ARROSTINO ANNEGATO (*Captain of the Tamorras—a Secret Society*).
GIORGIO RAVIOLI ⎫
LUIGI SPAGHETTI ⎭ (*Members of his Band*).
ALFREDO (*a Young Peasant, loved by* ULTRICE, *but in love with* TERESA).
PIETRO (*Proprietor of a Troupe of Mountebanks*).
BARTOLO (*his Clown*).
ELVINO DI PASTA (*an Innkeeper*).
RISOTTO (*one of the Tamorras—just married to* MINESTRA).
BEPPO.
TERESA (*a Village Beauty, loved by* ALFREDO, *and in love with herself*).
ULTRICE (*in love with, and detested by* ALFREDO).
NITA (*a Dancing Girl*).
MINESTRA (RISOTTO's *Bride*).

Tamorras, Monks, Village Girls, &c.

ACT I.—Exterior of Elvino's Inn, on a picturesque Sicilian pass. Morning . . . . . MR. RYAN

ACT II.—Exterior of a Dominican Monastery.
Moonlight . . . . MR. RYAN

DATE.—EARLY IN THE NINETEENTH CENTURY

The opera produced under the musical direction of MR. IVAN CARYLL.

composed works of higher pretension, among them being a Symphonic
Suite for orchestra, and the cantata *Gray's Elegy*, written for and produced at the Leeds Festival in 1893. He was a born melodist, and
although some of his works may lack dramatic grip on the one hand,
and the *vis comica* on the other, yet his tuneful and refined style was
always welcome alike to musicians and to the general public.'

Nothing could be better than the opening, which is brisk and sprightly, and introduces us to the business of the scene in a very effective fashion :

Chorus of Tamorras

We are members of a secret society,
 Working by the moon's uncertain disc ;
Our motto is ' Revenge without Anxiety '—
 That is, without unnecessary risk ;
We pass our nights on damp straw and squalid hay
 When trade is not particularly brisk ;
But now and then we take a little holiday,
 And spend our honest earnings in a frisk.

Solo—Giorgio

Five hundred years ago,
 Our ancestor's next-door neighbour
  Had a mother whose brother,
  By some means or other,
 Incurred three months' hard labour.

This wrongful sentence, though
 On his head he contrived to do it,
  As it tarnished our scutcheon,
  Which ne'er had a touch on,
 We swore mankind should rue it !

 . . . . . .

El. Bless my heart, what are you all doing here? How comes it that you have ventured in so large a body so near to the confines of civilisation? And by daylight, too! It seems rash.

Gio. Elvino, we are here under circumstances of a romantic and sentimental description. We are all going to be married !

Eʟ. What, all of you?

Lᴜɪ. One each day during the next three weeks. What do you say to that?

Teresa Miss Geraldine Ulmar.

Eʟ. Why, that it strikes at the root of your existence as a secret society, that's all. And who is to be the first?

Gɪᴏ. The first is Risotto, who went down to the village this morning, disguised as a stockbroker, to be married to Minestra. . . .

MR. HARRY MONKHOUSE AS THE CLOWN IN THE 'MOUNTEBANKS'

ARR. Good. We have a vendetta against all travelling
Englishmen. The relation of our ancestor's neighbour was
arrested by a travelling Englishman. Well?

GIO. No—very bad. The cowardly ruffian was armed.

MINESTRA   RISOTTO
Miss Eva Moore   Mr C
                           Burt

ARROSTINO
ANNEGATO

MR FRANK WYATT.

ARR. That's so like these Englishmen. This growing
habit of carrying revolvers is the curse of our profession.
Anything else?

LUI. Only an old market-woman on a mule.

ARR. Well, we have a vendetta against all old market-
women on a mule. The principal evidence against the rela-

tion of our ancestor's neighbour was an old market-woman on a mule. Did you arrest her?

Lui. We were about to do so, but she passed us in silent contempt.

Arr. Humph! This growing habit of passing us in silent contempt strikes at the very root of our little earnings. Of course you could do nothing?

THE DUKE AND DUCHESS

The change into clockwork figures furnishes the author with many quips and conceits:

Pie. Why, the duke and duchess want to buy the figures, and the figures are missing. What's to be done? Why, it's obvious. You and Bartolo dress and make up as the two figures. When dressed, you drink a few drops of the potion, diluted with wine (*tasting the cork and shuddering*). It's-- it's not at all nasty--and you will not only look like the two figures, but you'll actually *be* the two figures - clockwork and all!

MR. HARRY MONKHOUSE AS HAMLET, MISS AÏDA JENOURE AS OPHELIA, AND
MR. LIONEL BROUGH AS THE MOUNTEBANK

Ni. Whew! (*whistles*).

Bar. What! I become a doll--a dandled doll? A mere conglomerate of whizzing wheels, salad of springs and hotch-potch of escapements? Exchange all the beautiful things I've got inside here for a handful of common clockwork?

It's a large order. Perish the thought and he who uttered it ! . . . We are quite common clockwork, I believe ?

NI. Mere Geneva. The cheapest thing in the trade.

BAR. So I was given to understand.

NI. It might have been worse. We might have been Waterbury, with interchangeable insides.

BAR. That's true. But when I remember the delicately-beautiful apparatus with which I was filled from head to foot, and which never, never ticked—when I contemplate the exquisite adjustment of means to end, which never, never wanted oiling—I am shocked to think that I am reduced to a mere mechanical complication of arbors, pallets, wheels, mainsprings, and escapements !

.   .   .   .

NI. What's wrong now ?

BAR. I—c'ck—c'ck—I am not conversant with clockwork; but do you feel, from time to time, a kind of jerkiness that catches you just *here* ?

NI. No; I work as smooth as butter. The continued ticking is tiresome ; but it's only for an hour.

BAR. The ticking is simply maddening. C'ck ! c'ck ! There it is again !

Mr. D'Oyly Carte, on his side, made a gallant attempt to carry on the traditions of the ' Savoy.' In June 1891 there was presented a new opera, the words supplied by Dance, the music by Solomon. This was the ' Nautch Girl,' a rather brilliant spectacular effect, but of the usual comic opera pattern, familiar enough at other theatres. It introduced a very agreeable *cantatrice*, Miss Snyders, a singer of much grace and finish. There is something remarkable in the fertility with which the

United States have furnished quite a number of these pleasing and acceptable songsters, some of whom, like Miss Griswold, have even become leading singers in the Grand Opera at Paris—a situation so very difficult to attain when we consider how *difficile* and jealously exclusive are our neighbours. In spite of the comparative rudeness and provinciality of the American stage, these performers have an elegance and flexibility that is often lacking in the English singer. The secret may be that they nearly always have their training in foreign schools. In spite, however, of a magnificent setting, this opera was only destined to prove that there is an essential difference between the conventional 'opera of commerce' and the legitimate Savoy opera.

The manager also revived the 'Vicar of Bray,' the music of which, by Solomon, was recast. Later, he made a bolder venture with an opera written by a new and scarcely known musician, Ernest Ford. But he relied on his libretto, written for him by a professor of the so-called 'new humour,' Mr. Barrie, who is acclaimed by his countrymen as one of the prime wits of the day. This piece was 'Jane Annie.'

It is always interesting to speculate on the foundations of amusement, to ascertain what is really the genuine article, and 'see that we get it.' And as this little work is intended to be a sort of record of a particular form of humour that has long recreated the public, we will pause here for a moment to consider the claims of yet another method which was put forward as a substitute.

This new humour, or 'fun,' it seems to me, is but of a 'poorish' kind—Carlyle's word—and is, perhaps, founded on the free-and-easy familiarities used in irresponsible talk, or perhaps on an imitation of the jests in American newspapers. Such as it is, it is certainly not robust enough for the stage. Mr. Barrie is the author of many admirable stories and sketches of Scottish life and character, which have well deserved their great success. They are most racy and vigorous. *There* he was on his own ground, and might claim to be considered the best Scottish writer of the day. But this sort of native humour scarcely fits a writer for the delineation of English social peculiarities. He had previously written for Mr. Toole a piece for the stage, well-known as 'Walker, London,' the extraordinary success of which seems to be unaccountable. I can only say that though most catholic and receptive in all that concerns 'fun,' on the stage and elsewhere, I sat through this piece to the end, listening in amazement and bewilderment to the jests—statements, rather—of the characters. I have asked the opinion of sagacious critics, and most of them agreed with me that so far from seeing anything funny in it, they could not understand what was intended. It seemed to suggest

the simpering quips of some gentle curate surrounded
by a bevy of admiring ladies, and who might be heard
twittering, and saying of his schoolgirls, 'Mary Jane
is a nice, good little girl, but she wants *bringing out.*';
or, 'Thank you, I will have another cup, *if I am not
committing an excess.*'[1]

There are, of course, persons to whom the mere appearance of Mr. Toole on a houseboat is in itself an
exquisite jest, and a young university man in flannels
becomes a huge joke. There are many for whom the
production of a familiar object, such as a houseboat or a
hansom cab on the stage, gives intense delight.

Now, it may be repeated that there can be no question
as to Mr. Barrie's talents and even genius. I am only
noting a bewildering puzzle. But in this department it
must be said he has little notion of what true humour
is, and he here certainly supports the oft-repeated jest
as to the surgical operation, which has been so often
associated with his countrymen.

---

[1] Or perhaps, as another humorist sings in the *Mountebanks*:

> Though I'm a buffoon, recollect
> I command your respect!
>> I cannot for money
>> Be vulgarly funny,
> *My object's to make you reflect!*

> True humour's a matter in which
> I'm exceedingly rich.
>> It ought to delight you,
>> Although, at first sight, you
> *May not recognise it as sich.*

If ' Walker, London ' seemed flat and stale—though Mr. Toole did not find **it** ' unprofitable '—the piece ' Jane Annie,' contributed to the Savoy during the interregnum, was a more perplexing phenomenon **still.** Through the whole piece it was hard **to** see ' where the joke came in,' or what the writer intended, unless we accept the theory **of** the pet curate before alluded to. That this is no exaggeration will be seen presently.

Produced at the Savoy Theatre, London, under the management of Mr. R. D'Oyly Carte, on Saturday, May 13, 1893.

JANE ANNIE

OR

THE GOOD CONDUCT PRIZE

Written by J. M. BARRIE and A. CONAN DOYLE
Music by ERNEST FORD (with Explanatory Notes down the margin by ' Caddie')

Dramatis Personæ

A PROCTOR	MR. RUTLAND BARRINGTON
SIM } (Bulldogs)	{ MR. LAWRENCE GRIDLEY
GREG }	{ MR. WALTER PASSMORE
TOM (a Press Student) : . . .	MR. CHARLES KENNINGHAM
JACK (a Warrior)	MR. SCOTT FISHE
CADDIE (a Page)	MASTER HARRY RIGNOLD
MISS SIMS (a Schoolmistress) . .	MISS ROSINA BRANDRAM
JANE ANNIE (a Good Girl) . . .	MISS DOROTHY VANE
BAB (a Bad Girl)	MISS DECIMA MOORE
MILLY }	{ MISS FLORENCE PERRY
ROSE } (Average Girls) . .	{ MISS EMMIE OWEN
MEG }	{ MISS JOSE SHALDERS
MAUD }	{ MISS MAY BELL

One Night elapses between the Acts

Q

A page boy called 'Caddie' introduced a name presumably highly comic, as it is borrowed from the game of golf—a notion that seems to convulse all good Scots. This lad is made very precocious, assuming manly airs, &c. Dickens, it will be recollected, had the same character in Martin Chuzzlewit, who talks in exactly the same way. By way of adding to the 'fun' the comments of this youth on the incidents of the piece are supplied in the margin. The young ladies talk in this fashion:

ALL. A man!

ROSE. At last!

MILLY. Bald.

ROSE. The wretch!

MILLY. He has two other men with him.

MEG. Two! *Girls, let us go and do our hair this instant.*

And again:

MEG. What is Bab doing all this time?

MILLY. She has her ear at the keyhole.

MAUD. Dear girl!

MR. SCOTT FISHE AND MASTER RIGNOLD

MILLY. She shakes her fist at the keyhole.

ALL. Why?

MILLY. I don't know.

(BAB *comes upstairs.*)

ROSE. Bab, why did you shake your fist at the keyhole?

BAB. *Because it is stuffed with paper.*

The page boy here comments, 'If I had been Bab I would have had the paper out in a jiffy.'

BAB. That little sneak Jane Annie is not here?

MILLY. She has gone upstairs to bed.

BAB. You are sure?

ROSE. I'll make sure. (*Runs upstairs and looks through keyhole.*) It's all right, girls! *I can see her curling her eyelashes with a hairpin.*

MASTER RIGNOLD AND THE SCHOOLGIRLS

This seems laboured enough, and trifling too. Later someone is found 'fondling' boots!

Then the boy: 'Tom has wrote another play since then for the Independent Theatre. It is about a baby that was tired of life and committed suicide.'

JACK. But I am also a novelist—*at least I've—I've bought a pound of sermon paper.* Haw!

TOM. Well, I am also a dramatist. Why, I have a completed play in my pocket.

JACK. And a very good place for it too. Haw!

TOM. What is more, it has a strong literary flavour.

JACK. Don't be afraid of that. They'll knock it out in rehearsal. Haw!

JANE ANNIE

BAB

TOM. Nonsense. It's most original also.

JACK. That'll damn it.

TOM. Originality damn a play! Why?

JACK. Because ours are a healthy-minded public, sir, and they won't stand it. Haw!

TOM. It's an Ibsenite play.

JACK. Then why not produce it at the Independent Theatre?

Tom. I did.

Jack. Well?

Tom. And it promised to be a great success; but, unfortunately, just when the leading man had to say, 'What a noble apartment is this,' the nail came out, and the *apartment fell into the fireplace.*

What *can* be the point of the nail coming out and 'the apartment fell into the fireplace'? Withering satire on the luckless Ibsen, no doubt. But what is this to what follows?—

Jane A. (*hypnotising him*). You are my lover!

Jack. Darling! Haw!
　　　(*He goes to boat.*)

Jane A. I took that hole in two!
(Jane Annie *joins the others in boat. All wave handkerchiefs.*)

Proc. Hyp-hyp-hyp-

Chorus. -notise!

Miss S. Another!

Chorus. Hyp-hyp-hyp-notise!

Proc. One more!

Chorus. Hyp-hyp-hyp-notise!

MR. BARRINGTON AS THE PROCTOR

As I said before, Mr. Barrie is a clever man, and in his own department a genuine humorist; but it still remains an astonishing perplexing phenomenon how such things as these could be conceived, acted, or printed.

Such was this attempt at carrying on the humorous Savoy methods : with the result of showing what a startling contrast there was between the original and the attempted imitations.   On the first night all true Caledonians were convulsed with enjoyment, and roars of laughter were heard at certain golf terms—'niblick,' 'driver,' 'putter,' &c.—the mere mention of each being equivalent to a distinct witticism.

Towards the close of last year it became known that there were signs of a *rapprochement* between the estranged Savoy authors ; at this news there was general unfeigned satisfaction.   Once more audiences were to be recreated with the old form of entertainment of which the tradition only might have been left.   As it was, two years seemed a dangerously long interval; for in the stress and hurry of our time a capricious public is apt to forget its favourites and run after some new toy. Happily, however, nothing had appeared to distract it from what it had lost.   It was presently known that a reconciliation had been signed and sealed, and that the authors were once more busy together, contriving an entertainment of the old pattern.   The preparations went forward with the old animation and the old enterprise.

The *prima donna* on this occasion was a new American singer—one of the many who have figured at the Savoy opera, a person of graceful and 'prepossessing exterior,' as the papers have it—Miss Nancy McIntosh.

This lady proved to have a sympathetic though not very powerful voice. And she also has what has been happily described as 'that dainty finish of appearance' which seems to belong to most American girls.[1]

Mr. Gilbert has described to me the happy chance that led to this engagement. One of the most troublesome incidents connected with Savoy opera is the finding of the 'light soprano' who will be exactly suited to the scene. The well-trained, assured singer, practised in all the hackneyed existing devices, will not do. There must be a special freshness and grace, with even the refinement of inexperience. Earnestness, docility, sympathy, with sweetness and brilliancy of voice—such are the essential elements. The new singer was one of Mr. Henschel's pupils, and had already appeared at the Saturday Popular Concerts. At a dinner-party at this Maestro's—given, perhaps, not without a certain intention—Gilbert was struck with her singing, and more perhaps with her general style. After an interval she met

---

[1] On the eve of the performance she spoke of herself to a visitor in this chatty strain :—'Until something like a month ago I had never stepped on to a stage in my life; but I have taken very kindly to the boards,' she added, smiling, 'and, so far from being a weariness, each rehearsal was a pleasant experience. But that, I must confess, was greatly owing to Mr. Gilbert, who is the most delightful and painstaking stage-manager possible. I never knew so patient a man. After you have done a thing wrong twenty times, he will put you right the twenty-first as amiably as if he were telling you quite a new thing. I became word-perfect in a day and a half, thirty-six hours—of course, before I had even seen the score.'

him again, when he suggested that she should make a
trial on the stage before his colleague. She confessed
later that this was a nervous probation enough, singing
on the empty stage, the first time she had ever trod one,
and with so much depending on it. The result was
satisfactory, and she was engaged.

Once more the 'precincts' of the old Savoy were
in possession of writer and composer, now working
together to secure the best results for their efforts. The
curious fraternity of interviewers, or 'snappers-up' of
gossip, were furnishing such information as they could
extract, and everybody followed with intense interest the
stages of preparation.

A characteristic and unusual scene was the public
rehearsal, which took place on the night before the performance, in presence of an enormous audience. It was
a curious spectacle, the theatre being crowded by all
sorts and conditions of persons—artists busy with their
pencils, critics, and the many friends and acquaintances
of the management. The two or three front rows of the
stalls were vacant, and jealously guarded; and here the
author and composer appeared fitfully, wishing to note
the effect from this coign of vantage. The piece went
with extraordinary smoothness. Once or twice the author
or the composer interposed with a suggestion; but in a
general way the performance was identical with the
performance that was to be exhibited. At the termination

Gilbert, addressing the company, expressed the great pleasure with which he worked once more in association with the Savoy company, declaring his conviction that every part, even the smallest, would be played ' as well as it deserved, if not better.' He added his keen appreciation of the work done by Mr. Charles Harris, in his capacity of stage-manager; concerning which one may remark that 'Praise from Sir Hubert Stanley is praise indeed,' for Gilbert is himself one of the most *exigeant* of stage-managers. Three hearty cheers were given by the company for Mr. Gilbert, and then Sir Arthur Sullivan said ditto to Mr. Gilbert in a few graceful words.

This was an unusual scene, all the performers being drawn up in line to listen to the author and to the composer, who spoke from their stalls.

One of the most surprising and interesting features of this rehearsal was the perfect self-possession of the heroine, who went through all the complicated passages of her rôle as though perfectly familiar with the boards. After a long experience of the stage, I may say that I have never seen anything that approached this *tour de force*. Her voice was found to be flexible and pleasing, though perhaps scarcely strong enough for so high and difficult a part. In the grand *finales* and concerted pieces which close the acts, there is need of a strong and powerful organ to 'top' the rest. The more effective portion of her 'register,' as it is called, is lower down.

This might be considered one of the little romances associated with the Savoy. As the young American moved through her part in her graceful dress, she won all sympathies, which she was destined to retain during the long 'run.'

The piece is written in the best 'Gilbertian' manner, being a sort of fairy-tale brought up to date, full of sparkling jests and allusions.

'There are the two wise men who have hitherto ruled the King, both of them in love with Princess Zara, who is secretly engaged to a young soldier. The monarch sighs after Lady Sophy, the duenna, who would wed him but for the awful tales told by him, under compulsion, of himself in "The Palace Peeper." There is the artful Mr. Goldbury, who has succeeded in forming the whole country into a limited liability company, and thereby "put out of joint" the noses of the two wise men and their ally, the Public Exploder. We have also the tremendous effect of the sudden imposition on a semi-barbaric nation of English customs and laws. These are factors enough, with the aid of Mr. Gilbert's topsy-turvy logic, to lead to some wonderful and diverting complications.

'Immense prosperity comes to the country; therefore a plot is made by the discontented wise men, of whose love affairs nothing is heard after the first act, with the Public Exploder to persuade the people " that what they

supposed to be happiness was really unspeakable misery"
by swearing an affidavit to that effect. However, it
was carried out, the people were convinced, rebelled
against the King, and ordered him to send away his new
advisers. Then came the *dénoûment*. The people were
discontented with their prosperity; they wanted something else. Then the heroine said, "Why, I had forgotten the most important, the most vital, the most
essential element of all—Government by party!"'

One can readily pick out dozens of purely Gilbertian
turns: 'His Majesty, in his despotic acquiescence with
the emphatic wish of his people'; 'As there is not a
civilised king who is sufficiently single to realise my
ideal of abstract respectability'—is not 'sufficiently
single' a happy touch? 'Why, the fact is that in the
cartoons of a comic paper the size of your nose varies in-
versely as the square of your popularity.' '"Oh, yes!"
is but another and a neater form of "no."' There is the
quaint speech of Zara in reference to bad singing: 'Who
thinks slightingly of the cocoa-nut because it is husky?'

Nor is it only in witty phrases and brilliant comic
songs that the author has been successful. His treatment of the two younger sisters, who are trained as
models of propriety and exhibited, is very funny, and
every one of their scenes caused hearty laughter, to
which the demure acting of Miss Emmie Owen and
Miss Florence Perry greatly contributed. Moreover, the

Life Guards were very drolly handled, and most of the scenes between Scaphio and Phantis were exceedingly funny and very well played by Messrs. Denny and Le Hay.

First performed at the Savoy Theatre, London, under the management of Mr. D'Oyly Carte, on Saturday, October 7, 1893.

UTOPIA (LIMITED)

OR

THE FLOWERS OF PROGRESS

𝔇ramatis 𝔓ersonæ

KING PARAMOUNT THE FIRST (*King of Utopia*)	MR. RUTLAND BARRINGTON
SCAPHIO ⎱ (*Judges of the Utopian Supreme* PHANTIS ⎰ *Court*)	⎰ MR. W. H. DENNY ⎱ MR. JOHN LE HAY
TARARA (*the Public Exploder*)	MR. WALTER PASSMORE
CALYNX (*the Utopian Vice-Chamberlain*)	MR. BOWDEN HASWELL

IMPORTED FLOWERS OF PROGRESS

LORD DRAMALEIGH (*a British Lord Chamberlain*)	MR. SCOTT RUSSELL
CAPTAIN FITZBATTLEAXE (*First Life Guards*)	MR. CHARLES KENNINGHAM
CAPTAIN SIR EDWARD CORCORAN, K.C.B. (*of the Royal Navy*)	MR. LAWRENCE GRIDLEY
MR. GOLDBURY (*a Company Promoter*) (*afterwards Comptroller of the Utopian Household*)	MR. SCOTT FISHE
SIR BAILEY BARRE, Q.C., M.P.	MR. ENES BLACKMORE
MR. BLUSHINGTON (*of the County Council*)	MR. HERBERT RALLAND
THE PRINCESS ZARA (*Eldest Daughter of King Paramount*)	MISS NANCY McINTOSH
THE PRINCESS NEKAYA ⎱ (*her Younger* THE PRINCESS KALYBA ⎰ *Sisters*)	⎰ MISS EMMIE OWEN ⎱ MISS FLORENCE PERRY
THE LADY SOPHY (*their English Gouvernante*)	MISS ROSINA BRANDRAM
SALATA ⎫ MELENE ⎬ (*Utopian Maidens*) PHYLLA ⎭	⎧ MISS EDITH JOHNSTON ⎨ MISS MAY BELL ⎩ MISS FLORENCE EASTON

ACT I.—A Utopian **Palm Grove**　　　} Mr. Hawes Craven
ACT II.—Throne **Room in King**　　　} (by permission of
　　Paramount's Palace　　　　　　　 } Mr. Henry Irving)

Stage Director . . . Mr. Charles Harris
Musical Director . . Mr. François Cellier

Stage Manager, Mr. W. H. Seymour. The Dances arranged by Mr. John D'Auban. The Utopian Dresses designed by Mr. Percy Anderson, and executed by Miss Fisher, Mdme. Auguste, and Mdme. Léon. Uniforms by Messrs. Firmin & Sons, also by Mr. B. J. Simmons and Messrs. Angel & Sons. The Presentations by Mdme. Isabel Bizet-Michau. The Court Dresses by Messrs. Russell & Allen. The Judges' Robes by Messrs. Ede & Son. The Ladies' Jewels by The Parisian Diamond Company. The Wigs by Mr. Clarkson. The Properties by Mr. Skelly. Stage Machinist, Mr. P. White.

*The Opera produced under the sole direction of the Author
and Composer.*

It was indeed surprising, when one considers the sustained drain upon the author's invention, what a variety of effective quips and situations were here. The notion of a Utopian kingdom was in itself a stimulant to the fancy. The Utopian king is buoyant and eccentric enough; the other characters, numerous as they are, are all distinctly marked and quaintly exuberant. Nothing is better than the rough bluntness of the soldiers, with their intrusive 'First Life Guards':

I'm the eldest daughter of your king.

TROOPERS
And we are her escort—*First Life Guards !*
On the Royal yacht,
　When the waves were white,

In a helmet **hot**
  And tunic tight,
And our **great** big boots,
  We defied the storm :
For we're **not** recruits,
  · And his uniform
A well-drilled trooper ne'er discards—
And we are her escort—*First Life Guards !*

ZARA

These gentleman I present **to you,**
  The pride and boast of **their** barrack-yards ;
They've taken O such care of me !

TROOPERS

For we are her escort—*First Life Guards !*

FULL CHORUS

Knightsbridge nursemaids—serving fairies—
Stars of proud Belgravian **airies** ;
At stern **duty's** call you leave them,
Though **you know** how that **must** grieve **them** !

ZARA

Tantantarara-rara-rara !

CAPTAIN FITZBATTLEAXE

Trumpet-call **of** Princess Zara !

CHORUS

That's trump-call, and they're all trump cards—
They are her escort—*First Life Guards !*

Here the music **exactly** conveyed the soldierly bluntness of the corps, **which** though labelled 'Chorus ' had
a **distinct** individuality, **as** though **they** were characters

MR. RUTLAND BARRINGTON AS THE KING IN 'UTOPIA (LIMITED)'

in the drama.   These rhymes are quaint and ingenious :

> O make way for the Wise Men !
>   They are prizemen—
>   Double-first in the world's university !
> For though lovely this island,
>   (Which is *my* land,)
>   She has no one to match them *in her city.*
> They're the pride of Utopia—
>   Cornucopia
>   Is each in his mental fertility.
> O they never make blunder,
>   And no wonder,
>   For they're triumphs of infallibility !

One of the most diverting passages was the humorous
presentment of the tenor, found in every opera, who has
to carry on tender love-making to the heroine and at
the same time look carefully to his ' C in alt '—a matter
of arduous physical exertion.   The singer no less happily
carried out the idea than did the author and composer :

> RECIT—FITZBATTLEAXE
>
> Oh Zara, my beloved one, bear with me !
> Ah do not laugh at my attempted C !
> *Repent not, mocking maid, thy girlhood's choice—*
> *The fervour of my love affects my voice !*
>
> A tenor, all singers above,
>   (This doesn't admit of a question),
>   Should keep himself quiet,
>   Attend to his diet
>   And carefully nurse his digestion

MR. W. H. DENNY
MR. CELLIER   SIR ARTHUR SULLIVAN   MRS. D'OYLY CARTE   MR. D'OYLY CARTE
MRS. GILBERT   MR. W. S. GILBERT   MISS F. FER
MISS E. OWEN

MR. W. S. GILBERT READING 'UTOPIA (LIMITED)' TO THE

MR. W. H. SEYMOUR   MISS BRANDRAM   MR. GRIDLEY   MR. PASSMORE
F. PERRY   MR. RUTLAND BARRINGTON   MR. C. KENNINGHAM
    MR. C. HARRIS   MISS NANCY McINTOSH   MR. SCOTT FISHE

THE ACTORS AT THE SAVOY THEATRE

> But when he is madly in love
> It's certain to tell on his singing—
> You can't do chromatics
> With proper emphatics
> When anguish your bosom is wringing!
> When distracted with worries in plenty,
> And his pulse is a hundred and twenty,
> And his fluttering bosom the slave of mistrust is,
> A tenor can't do himself justice.
> *Now observe*—(*sings a high note*),
> *You see, I can't do myself justice!*

One of the characters, carrying out the precedent of the 'Lord High Executioner' in the 'Mikado,' is dubbed 'Lord High Exploder'; but the humour is somewhat mechanical. Gilbert has a curious partiality for such forms as this:

CAL. My Lord, I'm surprised at you. Are you not aware that his Majesty, in his *despotic acquiescence with the emphatic wish of his people*, has ordered that the Utopian language shall be banished from his court, and that all communications shall henceforward be made in the English tongue?

TARARA. Yes, I'm perfectly aware of it, although—(*suddenly presenting an explosive 'cracker'*). Stop—allow me.

CAL. (*pulls it*). Now, what's that for?

TARARA. Why, I've recently been appointed Public Exploder to his Majesty, and as I'm constitutionally nervous, I must accustom myself by degrees to the startling nature of my duties. Thank you.

The effect of such sallies on the audience—they are generally received with a puzzled expression—would be

R

a test of their value.   Sometimes, too, we find an in-
equality in the humour, as in this passage :

LADY SOPHY.   Actuated by this humane motive, and
happening to possess respectability enough for six, I consented to confer respectability enough for four upon your
two younger daughters—but although, alas ! I have only
respectability enough for two left, there is still, as I gather
from the public press of this country, a considerable balance
in my favour.

Or again :

ZARA.   But perhaps the most beneficent change of all
has been effected by Mr. Goldbury, who, discarding the ex-
ploded theory that some strange magic lies hidden in the number
seven, has applied the limited liability principle to individuals,
and every man, woman, and child is now a company limited,
with liability restricted to the amount of his declared capital !
There is not a christened baby in Utopia who has not already
issued his little prospectus !

This seems rather too involved, if not laboured, for
the stage, and at least must ' go over the heads ' of
audiences.   The old Scaphio's description of his love is
excellent :   ' When *I* love it will be with the accumulated
fervour of sixty-six years.'   This is witty from the
suggestion that age and experience—usually thought to
be disabilities in love affairs—are put forward as
recommendations.   His friend's ardour is amusing, too :
' *Though* but fifty-five, I am an old campaigner in the
battlefields of love.'

Gilbert's wit is not the wit of things or characters ; it might be called the wit of phrases and words. He is almost the first to invent methods in which the very form of a sentence becomes effective. There was something new and ingenious in this notion. In the same spirit he will use some familiar colloquialism with earnestness as the natural reply to something exciting or tragic. This is totally different from the 'mock heroic' of burlesque. I have shown that our author objects to the compliment of there being anything 'Gilbertian' in his humour. He probably might say that there is but one humour. But the distinction made, I think, meets his case.[1]

The old notion of the 'Duke of Plaza-Toro, Limited' is here developed :

PHAN. (*breathless*). He's right—we are helpless ! He's no longer a human being—he's a corporation, and so long as he confines himself to his articles of association we can't touch him ! What are we to do ?

SCA. Do ? Raise a revolution, repeal the Act of sixty-two, reconvert him into an individual, and insist on his immediate explosion !

---

[1] Our humourist once declared Wycherley's *Country Girl* to be 'preposterous rubbish.' This judgment I give up as incomprehensible, save, perhaps, on the ground that the humour has nothing verbal. Any one who has seen the *Country Girl* acted with spirit, must have seen a bit of real life and genuine character that will never leave his memory. Though it is ten years since I saw it, I seem to have known Moody and his ward in the flesh.

There are some piquant rhymes, witness :

> I'll row and fish,
>   And gallop, soon—
>   No longer be a prim one –
> And when I wish
>   To hum a tune,
>   It *needn't be a hymn one* ?

The author occasionally drops into a sort of political satire, which was also a well-known weakness of Dickens ; but it is scarcely in harmony with the light banter of the rest, such as Zara's recipe :

ZARA. Government by party ! Introduce that great and glorious element—at once the bulwark and foundation of England's greatness—and all will be well ! No political measures will endure, because one party will assuredly undo all that the other party has done ; inexperienced civilians will govern your army and your navy ; no social reforms will be attempted, because out of vice, squalor, and drunkenness no political capital is to be made ; and while grouse is to be shot, and foxes worried to death, the legislative action of the country will be at a standstill. Then there will be sickness in plenty endless lawsuits, crowded jails, interminable confusion in the army and navy, and, in short, general and unexampled prosperity !

When the king asks if the drawing-room arrangements are all correct—' We take your word for it that this is all right. You are not making fun of us ? This is in accordance with the practice at the Court of St. James's ? ' the Lord Chamberlain happily replies, ' Well, it is in accordance with the practice at the Court of St. James's Hall '—a hit that causes a general roar. ' Oh ! It seems odd,' says his Majesty, taking his seat ; ' but never mind.' And then follows a capital topical song legitimately suggested by the situation :

KING

Our Peerage we've remodelled on an intellectual basis,
Which certainly is rough on our hereditary races—

CHORUS

We are going to remodel it in England.

KING

The brewers and the cotton lords no longer seek admission,
And literary merit meets with proper recognition—

CHORUS

As literary merit does in England.

KING

Who knows but we may count among our intellectual
    chickens
Like you, an Earl of Thackeray and p'r'aps a Duke of
    Dickens—
Lord Fildes [1] and Viscount Millais (when they come) we'll
    welcome sweetly—

CHORUS

In short, this happy country has been Anglicised completely!

The opera was equipped with no less than three tenors—Keningham, Scott-Fishe, and Scott-Russell.

---

[1] Mr. Fildes, thus selected from his brethren, ought to be gratified at his public compliment.

The former, somewhat 'robustious' in tone, discharged his character with good effect. Scott-Fishe was more of the baritone, and had two effective songs, one in praise of the English girl, 'married,' as it should be, to an effective and sportive air :

SONG—MR. GOLDBURY

A wonderful joy our eyes to bless,
In her magnificent comeliness,
Is an English girl of eleven stone two,
And five foot ten in her dancing shoe !
    She follows the hounds, and on she pounds—
        The 'field' tails off and the muffs diminish—
    Over the hedges and brooks she bounds
        Straight as a crow, from find to finish.

    At cricket, her kin will lose or win—
        She and her maids, on grass and clover,
    Eleven maids out—eleven maids in—
        And perhaps an occasional 'maiden over' !
Go search the world and search the sea,
Then come you home and sing with me
There's no such gold and no such pearl
As a bright and beautiful English girl !

This is a pleasing sketch, and may be read with interest. Not less effective was the humorous financial song, declaimed with much spirit.

For brilliancy and all but dazzling show the piece surpassed all that had been hitherto attempted at the theatre. The dresses, lights, and general glitter were really extraordinary. The gorgeous 'drawing-room scene,' with its vast parquet floor, the 'surprise' of the Christy Minstrel performance, the glittering processions —all these were set forth in the richest and most costly style.

The most interesting incident of the opening night was the appearance at the triumphant close of the two authors, hand in hand : whose reconciliation was heartily acclaimed. Since that night the piece has been followed by vast audiences, and has had an even more prosperous course than any of its predecessors.

Such is a review of this pleasant contribution to the public stock of harmless pleasure. Our authors have certainly increased the gaiety of the nation. Our Offenbach and Meilhac have furnished us with a standing entertainment, all 'within the limits of becoming mirth.'

.   .   .   .   These merry men
Have joined their wits to make the general sport,
With nimble stroke shoot back the flying ball,
Nor let it touch the earth.

NOTE

It may be mentioned here that the 'Bab' Ballads, so often quoted and alluded to, owe their title to a sort of child's pet name given to the author, possibly an abbreviation of 'Baby.' Casting about for a suitable *nom de plume*, this occurred to him, and he adopted it, just as Dickens recalled the old childish name 'Moses,' which became 'Bozes,' and finally 'Boz.'

THE END

PRINTED BY
SPOTTISWOODE AND CO., NEW-STREET SQUARE
LONDON

www.ingramcontent.com/pod-product-compliance
Lightning Source LLC
Chambersburg PA
CBHW020349030726
47496CB00007B/2071